Unsuspected

Dolores Borrego Jacobs

Cordero Books, LLC are available for order through
Ingram Press Catalogues

Dolores Borrego Jacobs

Visit my website at www.doloresbjacobs.com

Printed in the United States of America First Printing:
September 2015 Published by Sojourn Publishing, LLC

ISBN: 978-1-62747-159-6
eBook ISBN: 978-1-62747-160-2

Inspired by the West Mesa murders,
all people, places and events
in this story are fictitious,
with exception of Felix Silva and
Silva's Saloon, San Bar Construction,
and the remains of 11 murdered
women—those are real.

Acknowledgments

I owe a debt of gratitude to my friends and members of the Knoxville Writers Workshop: Pat, Larry, David, Kay, and Anne for inspiring me to keep writing although years and miles separate us now. Thanks go to Charles Poling, an amazing writer in his own right, who encouraged me to finish my novel, but I don't think he expected me to write a second one before finishing the first. My thanks go to Morgan McArthur, DVM, for nearly running me over with his enthusiasm and motivation. I am especially grateful to my family who has supported my writing in ways too many to count. Finally, I offer a little prayer of thanks to my sister, Carmen, my mother, Teresa, and my great-grandmother, Celsa, who nurtured and challenged me — gone now, they were the strongest, most beautiful women I've known.

1.

ALBUQUERQUE STREETS IN 2003 are dark late at night in some parts of town. Central Avenue is like any of them except on the east end beyond Washington Street. There the alleys are full of lights, teeming with people strolling and wandering about, spilling out along the strip. The place has all the trappings of a bigger city. Neon signs with broken elements flash along the street. Doorway loiterers, drunks, drug users and sellers are abundant. Dogs rummage through trash and occasionally issue a yelp as a foot strikes one on the butt.

"Ged ouda heah," snarls a gravelly voice from the shadows where a dog is trying to lick something in a paper bag.

Streetwalkers lean against the walls of store fronts or stand by the street lights smoking cigarettes. Occasionally one pulls up on her short skirt to scratch an itch somewhere on the back of her thigh, cursing when she discovers a hole torn in her stocking.

The air in that part of town is heady. Car exhaust mingles with a sickening sour smell of garbage, the sweet weedy aroma of marijuana, and the pungent stink of old urine. Occasionally, a group of night clubbers enveloped in smoke walks the street to the next rendezvous talking loudly and laughing, perfuming the air with the scents of

English Leather and Pink Sugar. No one on the street bothers them. Safety in numbers, they think.

Toward the darker end of the strip, a few cars drive by quickly on their way to somewhere else. A dark blue older model Toyota sedan comes through there, not in such a hurry. The driver rolls the window down just a few inches for air and scans the street along the north sidewalk. In a few seconds, he spots a woman leaning against the end of the wall where a chain link fence ends and the building begins. She's about five feet tall and has dark hair. Her legs are shapely below her mini skirt.

He drives past her to get a better look then continues up the street as though he has other business. He goes on his way slowly but with an eye out for the side street up ahead where he turns right. Rounding the block he comes back up the street again. This time he stops in front of the place where the girl is standing. He lowers the window the rest of the way and softly calls out to her.

"Hey, there, can I ask you a question?" he says. She looks at him and walks toward the car.

"Need directions?" she asks. Her face is now closer to the window as she ducks to see him better.

"Not exactly." His warm, generous smile, dark hair and disarming looks momentarily put her at ease.

"Then, what?" She puts her hand on the car but still keeps her distance.

"Well, it's kind of embarrassing," he says.

"Oh, you're one of those guys who don't like to ask for help. Is that it?" She smiles at him and the corner of her mouth turns up in a teasing smirk.

"No, it's not that. I know my way around okay. It's just that I've never been with one of you girls before," he said. "You know."

"Sure. One of us girls," she says and gives a soft disparaging snort.

"Honest," he says. "I'm from out of town, and I don't know anybody here. I'd just like for you to sit with me–just to talk?" He smiles at her with a broad smile that shows his white teeth. She looks at him suspiciously.

"Yeah that's what they all say." She considers his offer.

"Oh, I get it," he says leaning over to reach for his wallet. "Look, I'll pay you for your time. You don't have to do this for free."

The girl shrugs her shoulders and walks around to the passenger's side. She pulls the door open and stoops to look inside. She can see that he's wearing casual clothes, a shirt with a button-down collar, a pair of blue jeans – and he smells clean. This guy's going to be different from some others she's had before. She feels less guarded.

"OK," she says and gets into the car.

He looks at her for a moment and smiles again. "Can we go somewhere quiet to talk? I know just the place. I saw it coming into town. It's not that far."

"I guess so," she said.

"Great." He starts the car moving slowly up the street. As he rounds the corner ahead, he speeds up to get through a residential area, then drives out to the highway and turns west.

"Where are we going?" She's beginning to feel her stomach tighten; she's apprehensive.

"Not to worry," he tells her. "It's a little place covered with trees, not too far from some houses. We'll be there in a minute."

A mile later, he pulls off the highway onto a dirt road that seems to go nowhere. He drives slowly until he comes to a lane that's flanked on both sides by a line of tall Trees of Heaven and willows. Those trees usually grow near the irrigation *acequias*, but there's no water in the ditches now. He pulls far into the lane and turns off the engine.

"What do you think?" he says, gesturing toward the view. The car is parked facing the opening of a broad mesa with a view of the western horizon. The stars are beginning to grow bright as the last light fades from the sky. There are a few clouds gathering overhead and a balmy breeze wafts into the partially open windows of the car.

"You hungry?" he asks.

"For what? I don't see any Lotaburger out here." She laughs.

"Oh, but you're wrong," he says and reaches around to the back seat for a plastic bag containing some French fries. He pulls open the bag and the mouthwatering smell of fried potatoes and salt quickly fills the car. He offers it to her.

"Where did you find these?" she says, eyeing the offer; surprised at how good the fries smell. She reaches into the bag.

"Save me one," he says, laughing.

Her eyes crinkle at the corners and she laughs like a school girl. She takes a couple more and settles comfortably into the seat to eat them.

"You know what?" he says. "This reminds me of prom night. I only went once when I was a junior in high school, but it was the best night of my life."

She turns to look at him. "What did you do on prom night?" she asks, poking the last fry into her mouth and licking the salt off each of her fingers.

"The prom was okay and afterwards we went to get some food at the drive-in. It was still early and she wasn't due back at her folk's house until eleven o'clock. So I suggested we go out to some quiet place and watch the stars.

"What happened?" said the girl.

"Everything happened," he says, pausing to remember, "except the sex. I didn't care. We necked and petted until the car steamed up and nothing could be seen through the windows. I liked kissing her and we lay on the seat of the car with our lips together while I stroked her breasts through her dress. I gave her a hickey just under the chin." He pointed to the spot on his own neck. "I was moving my hand down toward her pussy and we got so hot in the car that we almost couldn't breathe. Then things just stopped."

"What happened?"

"We got too serious and she started to squirm like she wanted to stop, so I did. I sat up and, well, my shorts were wet," he said ruefully.

"What did she do?" she asked.

"She straightened her dress, pinned her hair back up in some fancy way, and told me to take her home. So I took her home."

"Is she still your friend?"

"No, no, she isn't," he says, not quite regretfully. "You know what? I'm sort of turned on talking about this. Do you mind if I kiss you?"

She smiles and half reluctantly scoots herself toward him. He draws his face close to hers and talks slowly as his lips brush hers. She responds by putting her fingers gently up to his cheek.

"Let's get in the back seat so we can have more room. No buckets," he says, as he fumbles with the console. Eventually, he gets out and goes around to her side and opens the back door for her. She climbs in.

"That's better," he said as he pulls her close and puts his mouth on hers. She closes her eyes and leans back onto the seat. He carefully makes his way onto her body and begins moving against her upward, then back down in a slow rhythm. She leans into the pressure. He doesn't insist or rush anything but keeps his mouth on her lips.

"Is this how it was with your prom date?" she asks when he moves his lips to the side of her face and down to her ear.

"This is better than that," he says and slides his lips to her neck where he can feel her pulse throbbing like a drum.

"This is really amazing," she says, as she emits a semi muffled groan. Her body is becoming more receptive. "I know you only wanted to neck, but you've really got me turned on." She matches his movement and pulls up her skirt as he pushes her legs apart with his knee.

"Take off your belt and open your pants so I can touch you," she whispers.

He lifts his pelvis off of her to release the buckle and slides out the belt. He lowers the zipper. Her right hand makes its way down to his belly and lingers at the waistband of his shorts. Each time he moves, she moves her hand farther down inside his shorts. As his right hand goes up through her blouse to fondle her, the tiny buttons on her blouse open up and expose her naked breast. On the next upward thrust he puts his mouth on her breast and suckles her nipple. She moans as his hand goes up to her throat. Her neck is delicate and thin and his fingers can almost reach around it. He holds her neck and strokes it with each rhythmic thrust of his body. He imagines it's his penis he's holding, large and muscular with a life of its own. He strokes it firmly and rhythmically. His breath is furiously pumping like an engine.

He begins to climax. She reaches down into his shorts and grabs his short, stiff, pencil thin penis. She's momentarily perturbed by what she feels, but now her body stiffens as she tries to catch her breath and she involuntarily begins to spasm. He holds her throat tightly as she utters a strangled cry. His back arches and he breathes in short gasps. The more intense his effort the tighter he holds her throat. In a few seconds it's over. He lets out a deep guttural groan and then drops down on top of her, his heart pounding in his ears and chest.

"I'm wet," he gasps, lying on top of her. She doesn't respond. She isn't breathing.

Eventually, he looks at her face turned to one side, her eyes staring at the back of the passenger's seat. Her right arm is settled loosely on the floor. He notices the tiny pale mole to one side of her mouth and her black curly hair now flowing over the bench. He lifts himself off her body and pushes backwards out of the car.

When her remains are discovered on the West Mesa, she is thought to be the killer's first victim.

2.

LOS LUNAS IS A SMALL town about twenty-five miles south of Albuquerque along I-25 on one side and the Rio Grande on the other. The town was a proxy for the many small towns across the American southwest that grew up in the 1970s and 1980s. It was not as ethnically diverse then as it would later become, but there were Anglo, Hispanic and Indian people who mingled and worked together harmoniously. English was the primary language of most citizens thanks to public education, but the mixture of Spanish and Tiwa, the language of the Isleta Indian people, mingled with English throughout the extended families made for lively and colorful dialogue so typical of New Mexico.

Life in Los Lunas was tied to the land, and amenities were only a short drive away from a larger metropolitan area. Many people lived in clusters of relatives and close friends. One could say that this proximity began when the first settlers who received the Spanish land grants bought and sold parcels and collected in communities that grew by aggregation rather than by planning. Family life was important to the town residents, steeped in both religious and cultural traditions, they protected their way of life by keeping the community isolated from outside influences.

Later, as the generations left home, the town opened up and became a mecca for city people seeking a gentler lifestyle; they came from Albuquerque mostly, but also Edgewood and other places. Taxes were low in Los Lunas, and opportunity grew out of the urban migration from larger towns. Hubs of prosperity existed mostly in the business district along Main Street where car dealerships and local businesses were located. There were smaller thriving businesses such as the saddle maker, an iron works, a miller and a Farmers' Supply that grew out of the necessity and preference of farmers and ranchers to buy locally. There was the usual grocery store, several churches, a funeral home, a furniture store, one volunteer fire department and a small public library. During its development the town experienced the growth of illicit activity from gangs and drugs, but those enterprises lacked organization and most people were not affected by them day to day.

The Martinez family had lived in an older, more rural part of town since the 1980s. Their property included several acres of unevenly distributed lots where they and other family members and friends lived. Their home was a rambling old adobe built and added to by previous generations. It was cool in summer and warm in winter due to its thick mud walls. The layout lacked a central hallway, so rooms opened into each other with doors to protect what little privacy there was.

José Martinez, the head of the family; Viola, his wife who was pregnant; and their two children, Ramón and

Rosa, lived in the main house. José ran a *tienda*, a small store that stocked grain, sugar, some ranch supplies and a few comestibles. It was about fifty yards from the house, facing the road through town. It was not far from a Catholic church and nearer to a local bar. The family owned a couple of horses; one was an old nag that belonged to José's father and the second horse was used for the plow. Some goats roamed freely and kept the weeds from overtaking the property.

Life for this small extended family had remained unchanged for years. The grandmother and grandfather were in their seventies, considered old for their day, and lived across the yard in their own small place. José was well known throughout town and had built his reputation on the previously established reputation of his parents, but as an individual, he was not always liked by everyone. Viola had more close friends than José but knew her place in the home. Care of the home and property were a joint responsibility and José and Viola taught their two children how to work. Even at their young ages they washed dishes and floors, dusted the furniture and helped their father with chores outside. The children were obedient and well behaved, and never a source of concern to their parents.

Viola was a busy woman who took pride in maintaining the home by keeping the linoleum floors clean and waxed, the roof beams called *vigas* dusted, and the windows with many panes sparkling. She tended her red geraniums in the deep window sills on the south side and gave careful attention to a waxy leaf vine that filled one kitchen window and produced tiny clusters of white, velvety, star-shaped blossoms that had a fragrance reminiscent of gardenias. She cooked meals and ironed clothes for her family as well as linens for the nearby church. She regularly attended Mass on Sundays and Holy Days, and was frequently at the sunrise masses during the week. She exhibited her devotion to the church at home by strategically placed statues that included a large crucifix, the Blessed Virgin Mary, St. Joseph, St. Anthony, and a *nicho*, a recess carved into the adobe wall that held El Santo Niño de Atocha, a Roman Catholic image of the child Jesus. Tucked into the corners of a bedroom mirror were a small photo of Pope John Paul II and a smaller one of President Kennedy. She carried a rosary in her apron pocket and another in a coat that she wore when she went outside in cold weather. She was frequently heard softly reciting prayers to Mary and uttering beatitudes and invocations such as *Alabado los Dioses Nombres* and *Ave María Purísima*.

The garden behind the house, however, was truly Viola's domain. It contained an endless supply of medicinal herbs that she used for poultices, stomach remedies and salves. Some of her plants were impressive specimens like the comfrey with dark, arrow-shaped leaves forming a lush mound. Or the pale green *ruda*, a showy but toxic plant known as rue, that grew tall with small yellow flowers and rounded lacy leaves that green caterpillars would strip from the stems, if allowed. Mint spread from the garden to the ditch, sending ground covering runners in every direction. She had some herbs like rosemary, thyme, oregano, cilantro, sage, and dill that she used in her cooking. She groomed the garden assiduously. She also collected asparagus along the ditch in the spring and picked *quelites*, a wild edible plant that grew like a weed called Lamb's Quarters, to prepare with bacon and onions to feed her family.

Life for the Martinez family was simple. Friends and relatives thought Viola and José made a romantic couple because she was pregnant nearly every year. Yet they felt sorry for them because since Ramón and Rosa were born, Viola didn't seem able to carry a baby to term. This was a source of difficulty between Viola and José, but she tried hard to please him in other ways by cooking good meals, ironing his shirts, and being generally attentive.

The reality was that Viola had a troubling relationship with her husband. José was proud, arrogant and macho. He believed that a wife should be subservient to the husband. He considered himself superior to others because he was good with numbers and thought himself important in local politics. He had two passions: women, not necessarily his wife, and horses. He was frequently at the local races surveying the horse flesh, placing and giving advice on wagers, or in bars talking about gambling and politics. He drank when he won a race and his elation was shared among the men who bet on the winning horse. They slapped one another on the back, carried on in whoops and yells and fractured the air with rounds from their pistols.

When José lost a race, however, it was a much different story. He drank himself into a peevish state that escalated quickly into violence he carried back home with him. His wife was the primary recipient of his gin-fueled rages. Sometimes it was a beating but most often it ended in what amounted to rape. José resented his wife because she couldn't give him more children. He wanted to blame her, but deep down he wondered if the problem was with him. Drunken sex never calmed him for more than a few hours, so he went to the dances at the local bar and loitered outside in the parking lot hugging and kissing whatever woman he hooked up with. He frequently drove into Albuquerque or farther north for a game of poker at the more out-of-the-way joints. He was a big talker, liberal with his opinion, authoritarian in his tone, and accounted for neither his behavior nor his time to anyone.

José somehow managed to confine his binge drinking to the weekends, so during the week he was the good son and father. He was attached to his parents, Don Patricio and Doña Virginia, as they were called by everyone who knew them. Don Patricio was in his seventies, a product of the Depression Era, and he had seen his share of bad times as well as good. José spent time during the week working in his father's garden or helping him fix the barn or fencing. He was an only child and his father doted on him. José often worked on the old Chevy truck with his father, and it was during those times that their conversation brought them closer together.

Ramón and Rosa knew something about their father's behavior, yet they stayed close to him when he was working at home during the week. He in turn took them along to town when he needed supplies and bought them small tokens of affection; a hat with cherries on it for Rosa and a small pocket knife for Ramón were treasures to the children.

3.

ONE MORNING IN SEPTEMBER, José drove the Chevy pickup and trailer to Corrales and brought back a three-year-old sorrel filly named Red. She was a gentle thoroughbred-quarter horse mix with an elegance and grace that turned heads. He told everyone he bought her to take him into areas where his old pickup couldn't go, but his real plan was to make some money by competing in the local races.

The evening when he returned with the horse, José unloaded Red from the truck and tied her to the fence. Ramón and Rosa quickly found that her long legs made perfect poles where they could play tag. José saw that the horse remained perfectly calm but he didn't like for the children to play around her.

"Get away from the horse," he yelled at his children. They ignored him and continued their game.

"I don't want you playing near that horse! She could spook and kick you or step on you, hear me?"

"Why did you get her?" asked Ramón, finally giving up the game.

"I'm going to race her," said José.

"She's nice, Papá. Can I ride her?" asked Rosa moving closer to where her father stood.

"No, no," said José. "She's not a pony. She's a man's horse—a race horse," José said, as he hiked his pants up at the waistline and puffed up proudly.

"When's the race?" asked Ramón.

"I don't know yet. I have to talk to some men about it. Stay away from the horse, you hear?"

Ramón looked once more at the horse and obediently walked back to the house. Rosa hesitated, turned down one corner of her mouth and followed her brother.

After they were gone, José saddled Red and rode her out to the back of the property along the river. She handled well, and he was happy with his purchase. He had big plans for her.

José had his eye on a race about three weeks away. He was a good trainer but not a small man. He figured he could get one of his smaller friends to ride her for him. José tended to generate resentment from his friends and acquaintances; they found him pushy and arrogant but his arrogance made him an easy mark for a quick wager. Secretly they admired him because he was better educated than they, but he always let them know it.

"*Andale*, José, come on" said one of his friends. "Sign her up for next week. She looks ready to me."

"What do you know about horses, Samuel? The only race you've been close to was three feet from your TV during the Kentucky Derby."

"*Cómo eres pinche.* You're missing the boat, hombre," said Samuel, shaking his head.

"Leave me alone, Samuel. I'll decide when she's ready."

"Okay, okay, *No te enfades*, don't get mad," replied Samuel. "Just tell me when you're going to race her so I can bet on the other guy."

"*Mira cabrón*," said José, moving toward him with his fist raised.

"*Cálmate, patrón*. Calm down, boss. I'm just giving you a hard time," said Samuel, laughing and backing up with his palms forward.

"Get your hard times out of here, and leave me alone," said José, waving him off.

Later, José went to talk to his father about a race. Don Patricio shook his head when José told him that McAdams from the dairy was going to race his palomino, Montero.

"That horse is too big for your Red," he said.

"I think Red could take him," said José. "Montero's a fine horse but he's hard to handle."

"He's fast and unpredictable," said Don Patricio, thoughtfully. "You could lose everything in two minutes, hijo."

"I could win everything in two minutes, Papá," said José.

Don Patricio reached up and pushed his fingers beneath his hat to scratch his head.

"Where you going to get the money?" he asked.

"I have a little. Don't you want to get in on the bet?"

Don Patricio scratched his head again.

"I would like to," he said. "But you can't tell Virginia."

Doña Virginia, José's mother, had a calm demeanor but was known to be direct in her language. She still got around very well and was accused of having selective hearing.

"Patricio?" she said, from somewhere inside the house. "Don't be stingy with José. Give him some money."

"Yes, yes," said José's father. "Why don't you take him to the bank yourself, *Vieja*. You have more money than I do."

"Mira, Patricio. José works over here all the time and you don't pay him a nickel, you stingy old man!"

"¡*Basta*! Enough, mujer. I'm going to give him some money."

Don Patricio got up from the wooden chair on the long porch in front of the house, known in Spanish as a *portal*, and disappeared into the house. In a few minutes he returned with a tin of tobacco and sat down again. He pulled open the lid on the tin and withdrew some paper and a matchbook. A sweet, woodsy fragrance emanated from the tin as he pinched some of the blend and began to roll a cigarette. When he finished, he licked the edge of the paper and stuck it down. He set the cigarette on the arm of the chair to dry and reached for something inside his overalls. He handed a tight roll of ten-dollar bills to José.

"Toma, take this, José. If you need more, you'll have to get it out of your mother," he said loudly so she could hear him. He picked up the cigarette, put it to his lips and struck a match.

"Gracias, Papá," said José inspecting the roll before slipping it into his pocket.

The races were held on a dirt strip about five miles south of Los Lunas, roughly parallel to the highway. It was a straight quarter-mile track and lacked amenities like gates and flags. A couple of pallets with some plywood on top were set up for the announcer. A pistol shot would start the race and the man at the end of track with a line of sight to the fence post painted white, called the winner. Horsemen brought their impressive steeds from as far north as Taos and from Socorro, in the south. The event was carried by word of mouth with hours spent negotiating over the telephone. The purse was determined by how prominent the horse's owner was. Severino Trujillo, a wealthy businessman whose horses were well known, set the registration at seventy-five dollars. José had scraped together enough money to pay the entry fee with a little left over to place a bet.

On the day of the race, José pulled up in his pickup and trailer a few yards from the starting line. He unloaded Red, put the saddle on her and tightened the girth. About that time, his friend Fermín came forward from the parking area and took the mare's reins.

"She looks good, José. I'm pretty sure I can win this thing."

"Pretty sure won't win the race, Fermín," said José. "I've got money on this horse. Your skinny ass better fly across the finish line, you hear me?"

"Don't worry," said Fermín. "This one's in the bag."

"¡*Caballeros!*" called out a man from the platform, his hand raised with a pistol pointed to the sky. "We are ready to begin! Somebody, take those kids off the track!" he shouted and pointed toward some children who were chasing each other and spilling out from the crowd onto the track at every opportunity.

José handed over his horse to Fermín and moved up through the crowd to the railing. He stood at the half-way marker. The noisy crowd was leaning into the track so far that he could barely hear the nervous snorting and neighing of the horses over the racket. The announcer shouted something at the top of his lungs and then the gun went off. A few seconds later, the horses barreled along neck and neck past José, churning the track into a cyclone of dust. The golden streak of the palomino was slightly visible above Red's back.

As the horses bolted toward the finish, the crowd spilled onto the track to get a better look. A cheer went up. José squeezed through the wall of bodies, expecting to be congratulated.

"That Montero is one hell of a horse!" said someone to José's left.

"Did you see that mare? Looked like she was gonna win, but she got spooked or something," someone else said.

José ran full speed down the middle of the track to find Fermín already dismounted and walking Red around to cool her off.

"What the hell happened, Fermín? You told me you had the race won!"

"She ran pretty good!" Fermín replied. "I don't know what happened. She got spooked or something as we came up to the finish."

"You're not worth shit, Fermín. "I could have done better myself!"

"Come on, José. I ride your horse as a favor and this is how you treat me?"

"I should beat the hell out of you, *pendejo*." José accused his friend of being stupid. "I lost every penny I had on this race. Who's gonna make it up to me?" José yelled.

"You're a sore loser, José. Everybody knows it. It's a good thing my friends bet on Montero."

"What? What did you say, *cabrón*? You threw this race, didn't you? You skinny little fucker! What did you do, swing the *cuerda* across her eye?" José accused him, now seething. "I'll kill you, *jodido*!" he said as he moved toward Fermín in a murderous rage.

Fermín dropped the reins and took off running toward the parked cars where José lost sight of him.

"José!" Someone yelled. "Your horse is headed for the highway!"

José turned to see who was yelling and spotted Red heading back toward the trailer, loping alongside the highway. He quelled his rage as he desperately ran to catch his horse. Before he could reach Red, he saw a man cut out of the crowd up ahead of the horse and move toward Red to slow her down. The man grabbed her reins. When José realized that it was his father, humiliation stuck in his throat like the dust from the track.

4.

FRIDAY EVENING AFTER THE RACE, José sat at the supper table with his wife and their children. He had already been drinking and wanted to avoid thinking about the race and his humiliating failure. But he was still angry and wanted to fight. He began arguing with his wife about a dance she went to without him a few weeks earlier.

"Freddy tells me you are a great dancer, Viola. ¡Ese cabrón!"

"When did I dance with Freddy?" she asked, not wanting to encourage him.

"Who else did you dance with?" he said ignoring her question. "I suppose you slept with all of them, too," he said quickly escalating the argument.

"Why are you bringing this up now? I didn't sleep with anybody," said Viola.

"Like hell," replied José.

"For your information, I like to dance. Freddy asked me because he felt sorry for me."

"You're lying," said José looking at her enlarged body. "Freddy likes to get close and personal with women. Don't you have any decency but to go out looking like that?"

"It was a wedding, José. And where were you? Out behind the bar drinking with your buddies, as usual? Half those men resent you because you always dance with their

25

wives. But you never take me so they can dance with me," she said, not making eye contact. She pushed the food around on her plate with the fork.

The meal was nothing special, leftover beans and tortillas. The children were putting spoonsful into their hungry mouths and tuning out what seemed to them an ordinary dinner table conversation. José was becoming increasingly agitated, especially because he didn't really care that much about the accusation he was making, he just wanted to fight. He stood up abruptly, pushing his chair backwards onto the floor with a clatter. He reached into his pocket, pulled out a .22 caliber pistol and set it on the table. The children stopped eating, forks still in their hands. They slouched in their chairs, wide eyes shifting back and forth from their mother to their father.

"You make me sick," said José, twisting his mouth. He swung around toward the cabinet expecting to see a bottle on the counter. "What have you done with it?" he growled.

"It's just inside there," she replied, nodding toward the cabinet. "You've had enough."

"I'll tell you when I've had enough."

He reached into the cabinet and pulled out a nearly empty bottle of Gordon's gin. He preferred gin because it made him feel powerful. He removed the cap and tilted the bottle to his lips. After shaking the bottle to get the last few drops, he threw it into the corner where it shattered against the base of the cabinet. The children startled and screamed. José wiped his mouth on his sleeve and picked up the pistol. He turned unsteadily to Viola and savagely put the end of the barrel in her mouth. She looked up at him with a blank stare.

"No, Papá," cried Rosa. "Don't hurt Mama. Don't," she pleaded.

He glanced at his children then grabbed his wife with his left hand and jerked her out of the chair.

"Let's go," he said, holding the gun to her head as he pushed her awkward body out the door.

The children got up from their seats wanting to go to their mother. Rosa ran to her and grabbed her skirt, but Ray stood frozen in place.

José moved in a drunken charge down the road in the direction of the bar. He put the pistol into his belt so he could use both hands to drag his wife, and Rosa, who wouldn't let go of her mother's skirt. The afternoon sun had set but there was enough light to see by. It had rained hard in the early afternoon and the ground was muddy. Rosa's bare feet sank into the mud as she walked along clinging to her mother.

José entered the building on the south side, pushing his wife toward the far end of the bar. There were half a dozen men inside engrossed in their drinking and small talk. They looked up as he rounded the bar. By now his face was ruddy from exertion and rage. Viola was clutching her child's arm.

José pushed his wife against the bar. The child buried her face in her mother's skirt and began to cry. He ignored her sobs as he pulled out the pistol and aimed it at Viola's head.

"I'm going to kill her," he said. "I'm going to shoot her right here."

The men in the bar looked up and froze in mid drink. They slowly put their glasses down.

"José, don't do it, man," said a voice from among the tables.

"Shut up," José yelled. "Stay out of this. She deserves it for being a tramp, a *vagabunda*. How do I know she's not sleeping with you, eh?"

"Don't you be a fool," said another voice.

"I'm going to kill her right now!" he yelled.

Sitting in a small nook, partially hidden in the shadows at the end of the bar, was an older man nursing a small tumbler of wine. He'd been watching the situation and carefully keeping track of events. He was upset but not surprised by José's behavior. After all, he knew his son well. He watched José wave the gun at Viola and move closer to her. José tried unsteadily to get better aim. His hand was tight on the pistol and he talked rapidly as he kept adjusting his grip.

By now Viola was pale and staring at her husband.

"Go ahead and kill me," she challenged. "Kill us all," she said, placing her hand on her pregnant belly and looking down at Rosa. "Do it, *cobarde*," she said, calling him a coward.

José moved his finger onto the trigger and his face grew darker. His arm began to shake as he tried to keep the gun steady. At that moment, Don Patricio raised his arm from the bar with considerable force and pushed his son's gun-wielding hand up and away from Viola. The pistol flew out of José's hand without firing and he stood there dumbfounded. He looked at his father in surprise, then ran out of the bar blubbering. Viola remained standing, frozen and pale as death.

After a few seconds, Don Patricio slugged down the last of his wine, got up and recovered the pistol from the place near the window where it landed.

"Let's go Viola," he said, taking his daughter-in-law by the arm. "I'll take you and the girl back home."

"Fast thinking, primo," said someone from the back raising his glass in a sort of toast.

Another man laughed nervously.

"What a thing," said another, shaking his head and downing his drink in one shot. The men returned to their talking and drinking.

Ray remained rooted beside his chair until the sun set and the kitchen was almost dark. At last he heard voices outside and realized that his grandfather was with his mother and sister. He went to his room and laid on the bed. The light went on in the kitchen and he heard the reassuring voice of his grandfather say goodnight and the conversation between his mother and sister.

"Mama, can I sleep with you tonight?" Rosa asked.

"Yes, mija," Viola replied. "You go ahead and get ready for bed."

"No, Mama. I'm scared. What if Papá is in the house?"

"Don't worry, hija," said her mother. "He won't be back tonight."

Viola looked in on Ray to make sure he was in his bed.

"¿Hijo?" she called softly. He didn't answer but she saw his form on the bed and was reassured.

Ray lay with his eyes open, taking in the sounds. He didn't know whether to be upset with his father or with his mother. He didn't know whom to believe. He respected his father but also feared him. He wondered if his father was upset because his mother had actually done what she was accused of doing. Is that why he drank so much, and if so, perhaps he had a right to? Would his father actually kill his mother? Was his mother innocent and telling the truth?

He thought about the times when he took pleasure in his mother's affectionate ways. It was his habit to protest, saying that he was too old for that sort of stuff, but she teased him about being macho and said he'd always be her baby no matter how old he got. He learned that the less emotion he showed her, the more she came after him with her hugs. It was a game between them. Her attention took on a new intensity when she got pregnant. At first, it was easy for her to heckle him, but after a while, she had to reach for him around her growing belly, and he didn't care much for the way it felt when she pressed against him. It didn't matter now to Ray. He felt cold and numb inside, as if he had swallowed an ice cube and it stuck in his chest. Sometime between the voices of his mother and sister preparing for bed and the gnawing doubts that plagued him, he fell asleep.

5.

VIOLA SAT IN THE KITCHEN after Rosa and Ray were in bed. She felt drained of all emotion and stared through the window into the darkness at something far beyond. Her arm rested on the table and she stroked the grain of the wood over and over as though trying to smooth the imperfections there. She had a lump in her throat that she couldn't swallow and worked it nervously. There were no tears. She rose from the table and walked to the back room, where the telephone was located. She dialed the number of her friend and confidante Guadalupe Gabaldón. Viola had need of her professional advice. Her friend answered immediately and agreed to come by in the morning to see her.

Guadalupe practiced *curanderísmo,* a healing tradition that most likely started in Spain and among the native people of Mexico and survived for 400 years among the Hispanic settlers of New Mexico. She was stern and austere in her appearance. She wore black from head to toe with a shawl pulled over her head and a long gray braid hanging over her shoulder to the front. She wore a jute cord with a small cross around her neck. Despite the fact that the young boys in the neighborhood referred to her as "an old crow," she had a good reputation as a healer and the people in the community trusted her.

Guadalupe and Viola had a close relationship. Viola had been the first person in Los Lunas to welcome Guadalupe when she arrived from Jalisco, Mexico. She was undocumented but quickly assimilated among the more religious women in the village who found her knowledge of remedies and spiritual healing indispensable. The men were not as accepting, mainly because she didn't indulge their macho ways so they were at a loss to understand or influence her. Word among them was that she had been run out of Guadalajara, the capital of Jalisco, for practicing witchcraft. Closer to the truth was that she had been conducting medical diagnoses over the telephone for the sum of fifty dollars and was getting rich. Whatever her method, she was good at it, but some people feared her.

Viola found that Guadalupe had a calming effect on her, especially because she was so conflicted about her relationship with José. Once Guadalupe had heard Viola's story about violence at the hands of her husband, they bonded and began to share information that Guadalupe told to no one else. Guadalupe made it clear that she did not like José and would do everything she could for Viola, even to the extent of intervening to end an unwanted pregnancy.

Guadalupe arrived as promised early the following morning. Viola had made her a cup of coffee with three teaspoons of sugar, as she always requested. She carried a small leather pouch and placed it on the table next to the cup. She placed her right hand on the pouch and drank coffee with her left hand. She was *zurda* and being left handed was believed to confer special powers for healing to a *curandera*, a woman who heals people.

"*¿Qué pasa, mi amiga?*" She asked her friend what was happening.

"Guadalupe, José *me quiere matar*," said Viola.

"*¡Dios mío!*" said Guadalupe. "Why he wants to kill you?" Her English was sketchy.

"*Tú sabes*, it's the same thing. He gets *borracho* with that gin and he hurts me. Mira, look at how pregnant I am. He doesn't care about these babies he makes," said Viola, shaking her head in dismay.

"Ay, amiga. What I can do for you?" asked Guadalupe.

"*No puedo vivir así*, I just can't live like this, pregnant all the time. *Me tienes que ayudar.* Guadalupe, you must help me!"

"*Bueno, bueno. Cálmate. Aquí tengo un remédio en mi bolsita*," said Guadalupe wanting to calm her down. She opened the pouch and withdrew a vial of brown powder and held it out to Viola.

"What is this medicine?" asked Viola.

Guadalupe stared at her.

"Put a leetel of dees in your cup of ruda, *pero dar cuidado*. Works fast," she cautioned. "It make you seek for a few days, *luego terminas*. De babe no more. *¿Comprendes?*"

Viola held the vial between her thumb and forefinger and considered the option. Whatever was in the vial when mixed with ruda would cause her to miscarry. She and

Guadalupe gazed at each other for a long moment then she put the vial in her apron pocket, sealing her acceptance.

Their conversation had long since turned to gardening when Rosa stuck her head into the room and gave Guadalupe a little finger wave without saying anything, then disappeared outside.

"*Qué niña tan linda*," said Guadalupe. "A beautiful muchacha."

A pang of guilt swept over Viola but she quickly dismissed it. She was determined to stay with the plan. She had faith in Guadalupe, for she had used her skills many times in the past. The pregnancies she had aborted were early terminations and did not require anything special. She hoped this time would be the same. Whatever trepidation she felt about her action quickly dissolved as she thought about José and the gun. Maybe she'd be better off if he'd killed her, she thought. The morbid thought passed.

6.

RAY'S FATHER RECOGNIZED his son's potential early and made sure he went to school. Even when he was young, Ray already had a good mind for numbers. The skill came in very handy. Ray remembered details, understood how to fix things and knew something of construction. He had a sense of mechanics and could reassemble the parts of an old motor. He understood the uses for wrenches and their sizes, and could tell the difference between a straight end and a Phillips end screw driver. He was handy to have around when José worked on the truck. Most surprising to his father was Ray's knowledge of subjects like how to make adobe bricks. The summer that Ray turned thirteen, he helped his grandfather build a *soterrano*, a root cellar made of adobe.

As soon as school was out for the summer, Ray reported to his grandfather's house. He helped him assemble tools and equipment in preparation for the work ahead. Don Patricio borrowed an old backhoe from his neighbor to dig a hole at the back of his property. He wanted it to be six feet wide by six feet long. He dug the hole three feet deep anticipating the addition of adobe walls to raise the structure up to six feet. A roof would be added last. Don Patricio piled the dirt in one place so that it could be used to make the adobe bricks. He had salvaged a pile of two-by-fours that he cut and nailed to form ten-by-fourteen-inch ladder-framed rectangular boxes. Ray helped him lay out the frames in a quadrant with enough room to step around them. Don Patricio hooked an old trailer to the Chevy pickup and hauled a metal barrel full of water to the work site. He laid out a shallow, wooden, boat-like mortar box, some buckets, a cement hoe and some trowels near the frames. The last thing he did was to bring several bales of straw from the barn and cut loose the binding twine.

Ray's grandfather was an expert who worked steadily and quickly as he shoveled the clay and sand mixture from the pile into the mortar box. He added the right amount of water and crushed straw until he had achieved the soft mud consistency that he sought. He filled a bucket with the mud and directed Ray to put it into a frame. Ray did as he was instructed, making many trips until all the frames had been filled. His grandfather tapped the sides of the frames to get rid of voids in the mud and roughly smoothed over the tops. Several hours later, the bricks were dislodged from the frames, trimmed and left to dry. It took several weeks to make and dry the bricks. Meanwhile, Don Patricio scavenged some concrete blocks and laid them in around the sides of hole, stacking them up to ground level. He set the adobe bricks on these and raised the above-ground walls of the cellar. Once the structure was in place, Ray helped to set a roof across the walls, lay tar paper over the top, build a door, and then Don Patricio covered the entire structure with dirt until it looked like a mound. The only thing visible was the opening to the cellar.

Ray liked working with his grandfather. It gave him a sense of purpose. He was able to witness the product of his labor and take pride in his contribution. Ray's confidence grew as his grandfather called for him each day and praised him for his effort. When the project was completed, Ray took special satisfaction in knowing that his grandfather actually used the soterrano to store onions, apples and pumpkins for the winter.

One afternoon, Ray was tasked by his father to load some bales of hay from the barn into the pickup, so he could haul them out to the pasture. He had to do it alone because his father was tending to something else. Ray didn't mind because he was strong from his previous work with his grandfather. There was also that back-breaking work beside his father and the other men in the community during the early spring, to clear the acequias of tree roots and last year's debris, so the irrigation water could flow unimpeded. By comparison, forty-pound bales seemed easy to lift and toss into the back of the truck. He proceeded without complaining.

Pete Estrada, a childhood playmate who lived down the road, rolled up on his bike to see what was going on, as was his custom. He was a few inches shorter than Ray, and fatter. His spiked-up hair made him look a bit like a hedgehog.

"Hey, *vato*, how about you and me go ride our bikes down by the rio?"

"Take a look at this hay. Does it look like I have time to go riding to the river?" snapped Ray.

"Come on, *carnal*," said Pete, imitating the language of his older brother who was a gang member in Albuquerque. "I'm seeing my childhood pass me by with every one of those you load."

"Knock it off, Pete," said Ray, looking around to see where his father had made off to.

"Your old man has other things to do. He won't miss you for an hour. Besides, I need some help smoking these," he said, pulling a pack of Marlboros from his pants pocket.

Ray stopped loading the bales to catch his breath and consider Pete's offer.

"Oh, all right," he said. "But only for an hour. If my father finds out he'll beat the hell out of me."

"*Chingado*," exclaimed Pete. "We better get going."

Ray took a long look around once more, then retrieved his bicycle from the barn and joined Pete in a liberating race for the river. When they reached a sandy area on the bank they left their bikes and went straight to the water's edge.

"Can you believe we used to swim in that?" exclaimed Pete, looking down at the fast moving muddy water. "Remember that Chavez kid that almost drowned? You were fast, Ray. You and Tony jumped into that muddy water and pulled the kid out before he went under for the third time. That took *huevos*!" he said, as he expertly lit a cigarette and held the Bic lighter for Ray. They blew great clouds of smoke and laughed hysterically at a duck that was quacking and bobbing in the shallows for snails. Pete began coughing and laughing simultaneously. Ray was growing impatient. He took one more long drag on the cigarette and flipped it into the water.

"We got to get back," he said, as he straddled his bike and turned it around.

"It's only been fifteen minutes, vato! No fun," said Pete, shaking his head and grumbling as he continued to cough. "No fun at all." He reluctantly climbed on his bicycle and followed Ray.

When Ray and Pete arrived at the barn, José was waiting for them. He had loaded the remaining bales by himself and was angry.

"Get your asses over here," he lashed out at the boys. "You first, Ray. And don't even think about moving, Pete."

Ray paled as he approached his father. José slapped him on the back of the head then grabbed him by the collar and pushed him inside the barn. In a few minutes he returned for Pete. He didn't strike the boy but grabbed his arm and hauled him into the building. Ray was hanging by his feet from a rafter, his shirt down over his face and his hands unable to touch the ground. Pete yelled and tried to run but José had a strong grip on him. He grabbed another length of rope that was already looped over the rafter, tied it around Pete's ankles and pulled him three feet off the ground to about the same level as Ray.

"Please, Mr. Martinez," pleaded Pete. "My mama will be looking for me."

"Does your mama know that you come here to make a pest of yourself?" asked José.

Ray said nothing.

"I gotta go home, Mr. Martinez," said Pete trying not to cry. "My mother is expecting me for supper."

José ignored him as he made sure the ends of the ropes were securely tied to the barn posts and then he drove off in the truck to take the bales to the pasture.

"Shit," said Ray. "I told you he would be mad."

"Mad? Your dad is fucking crazy!" said Pete hysterically. "How long is he gonna keep us here?"

"Don't know," said Ray. Until it gets dark, I guess."

"What if . . . if I have to piss," stuttered Pete.

"Just don't open your mouth if you do," said Ray, seriously. Pete got the chuckles at the suggestion. Soon they were both laughing so hard that their ropes began to swing. Pete reached out and grabbed at Ray's sleeve. Ray responded by grabbing Pete's hand and soon they were swaying back and forth like a playground swing.

"Hey, Ray? What if the blood starts to run out of my ears?" said Pete, trying to catch his breath.

Ray looked at his friend whose face had turned red as a radish and considered the possibility.

"Nah, it won't happen but just in case, let's see if we can get down from here," said Ray. "Try to push me as hard as you can."

Pete grabbed Ray with one hand and pushed him with the other hand. As the boys began to move in unison their bodies became a pendulum. They looked around to see if there was anything to grab hold of, but Ray's father had made sure the ropes were long enough to secure them out of reach. Exhausted and dizzy, the boys came to a dangling halt.

"I've got an idea," said Ray. "Since you're smaller, grab hold of my clothes and see if you can pull yourself up to my feet."

"I don't see how that's gonna work, Ray," said Pete, his voice sounding more nasal than before. That's a trick for an acrobat, not a 'fat kid' like me," he said, suggesting that he had previous experience with that brand of name calling.

"Well, I'm probably stronger than you. I'll try it."

"Damn straight," said Pete, trying to sound tough.

Ray brought his upper body up and reached across to Pete. He grabbed onto Pete's legs at the top of the thigh and was able to pull himself up toward Pete's feet by pulling on his pants. He saw that Pete was wearing loosely laced high tops that seemed too big for his feet.

"Keep your hands down so you don't land on your head, Pete. I'm going to untie your laces," he said. He pulled on the laces and Pete's right foot slipped out of the shoe. Pete was hanging by the other foot.

"Hey! Ray. Take it easy! I think I'm gonna throw up," said Pete.

Ray managed to pull the laces loose on the other shoe and Pete came down with a heavy thump followed by his shoes. He sat up trying to recover from the fall and began to cry.

"Damn your father to hell," said Pete, beating the hay and dust off his head and body. "Crazy fucker almost killed me," he blubbered, as he rose unsteadily to his feet.

"Do you think you could untie my rope over there, Pete?" asked Ray twisting his head toward the post where the rope was tied.

Pete swayed a bit as he walked toward the pole. One firm jerk released the looped knot and down came Ray.

"I'm going home," said Pete in a daze. He didn't bother to ask Ray how he was. He grabbed his shoes and disappeared around the corner where he'd left his bike.

Ray sat and rubbed his elbow where it hit the ground. He stared out of the barn in the direction of the pasture. He wondered where his father had gone. He got up, shook the dust off his pants, and headed for the house. There was still no sign of his father, so he went inside to his room, pulled off his dusty clothes and crawled on top of the bedspread. He still tasted that Marlboro.

After the incident, Ray avoided his father and hardly made eye contact with him when he saw him. He continued to perform his chores, but he had no incentive. He wanted to ask his father why he had punished him and Pete in such a drastic way, but he knew his father would justify the behavior by saying that he needed to teach him a lesson. In Ray's mind, the punishment did not suit the crime. Instead, he began to read more and threw himself into his school work. Time passed, and things at home became tolerable again, but Ray could not recapture the former feeling of respect he'd had for his father.

7.

FOR SEVERAL YEARS RAY was harassed at school. He lacked social skills, so his only defense was to bury himself in schoolwork. He liked math because it was precise and predictive. He took comfort in a subject that not everyone liked or was competent in and made it his armor. Numbers offered him distance and control of his world. Over time the tenor of the abuse abated. Ray graduated from high school at sixteen, the year that Rosa was finishing her sophomore year. He started attending the University of New Mexico that fall. He was young to be at the University and couldn't relate to the more mature students. He wasn't interested in going to all-night keg parties down in the Bosque. He wasn't all that interested in ball games. He didn't much like the idea of dating. The language of business was what appealed to Ray. He had aptitude for translating anything with monetary value onto spread sheets and balance sheets. What was tangible or intangible in the accounting world put things into perspective in Ray's personal world. Accounting tabulated everything quantifiable. He grew up in a household where violence was unpredictable, but numbers were predictive and precise and gave him control and distance. He went home for the first long weekend in October.

Ray's mother started doing the laundry at six o'clock on Friday morning. She was pregnant again, didn't sleep well, and woke up tired. He heard her roll out the Maytag and start the water running with that characteristic sound as it flowed through the hose from the faucet to the machine. She was going to need help with the rest of the setup and sure enough, she called out to him.

"Ray! Are you awake? Go get your mama the tub from the barn," she called through his closed door. He'd slept nearly ten hours, yet not enough. He rolled over in the bed, facing the wall and pulled the pillow over his ear.

"Ray," she called again. "I need your help, hijo." She banged on his door. Ray knew this was laundry day in the household. The tub she wanted was for rinsing the clothes in cold water. It was Ray's job to fill it. He turned over half asleep and reluctantly swung his legs over the side of the bed where his shoes were.

"I'll take care of it, Mama!" he called out. His eyes watered and his throat burned from having slept on his back with his mouth open. He dug around in his closet for a clean shirt and pants, rubbed his hair hard with both hands to smooth it down a bit, and stood by the door buttoning the shirt. His mother was sitting at the kitchen table sipping some yellowish tea from a large mug. It seemed to Ray that she drank a lot of tea. She stood up, waddled over to him and grabbed his shirt sleeve.

"Why do you keep your door closed all the time?" she asked, looking up into his face. He was almost a foot taller than she.

"You hiding some secrets in there?" She tried to see around him into the room.

"No, Mama," he replied, bored by her feeble attempt to get information. He tried to get past her, but she was like a barrel standing in his way.

"Let me go, Mama," he said, taking her by the wrist and pulling her hand off his shirt. He sidled past her and went into the kitchen. As he stood before the sink he unscrewed the hose, turned on the tap until it ran cold, put his mouth against the faucet and drank directly from the stream. When he'd slaked his thirst, he stood up and wiped his mouth across his sleeve, then began poking around inside the cabinets.

"Isn't there anything to eat?"

"*Allá*," pointed his mother, "in the breadbox...some tortillas."

Ray let the breadbox door bang open, noticed the smell of stale bread and took out two, small, hard tortillas that had black circles burnt on them.

"When did you make these?" he asked, tapping the hard disks on the counter. His mother gave him a sad little smile.

"I haven't been doing much lately," she said and shook her head. "Last night when I couldn't sleep, I fried some eggs, but ended up throwing them in the trash." She lowered her head.

Ray looked at the miserable woman before him. Her face was swollen, and there were dark crescents beneath her eyes. It was hard for him to see the petite and lively woman with fair skin and fiery eyes she had once been. This was the fifth pregnancy that Ray could remember and he could see that her condition was sapping her vitality. What's more she was driving him crazy with all her carping. "Get this done! Get that done!" Even when he was eating dinner, she'd say, "Talk to me, hijo!" Some days he'd had more patience with her than others, but not today. He jammed a shard of hard tortilla into his mouth and walked toward the door. She took the opportunity as he was leaving to reach out and give him a hug around the neck, but lost her balance.

"What are you trying to do, Mama, hurt yourself?" he said, as he helped her regain her footing. He stood holding her arm while she caught her breath.

"What is it? You getting too old for your mama to kiss?" she chided.

Ray shook his head but didn't look at her. He squeezed her fat arm until her skin turned white under his strong fingers.

"Stop it, Ray! *Desdichado,*" she said, accusing him of having no respect for her. "Don't be like your father." Her voice was pained and circumspect, a voice that stirred up memories of things that frightened Ray in an imperceptible way.

"Men don't understand women," she went on as she sat down. "They don't know how to listen. They're just pretenders. Comforts come first with them. It turns them into animals," she said, swallowing and twisting her mouth as if she'd eaten something distasteful.

46

"You are a fine son, Ray, but you don't understand women," she said, as if predicting his future. "You think they are deceitful and treacherous, but you'll pursue them and use them just the same. It's the way things are between men and women." After her speech, she shook her head and stared down into her cup of tea.

Although he sought no disruptions in his relationship with his mother, his love for her had long ago turned to toleration and ultimately to indifference. He went through the motions out of habit and at that moment he wanted to squeeze her arm harder and drive the pained, animal look from her face, but he hated to hear her cry. He let go of her, knowing it was useless to talk to her about it. He left the kitchen but did not return with the washtub.

Ray's confusion wasn't confined just to his mother. He found all women confusing. He often heard his Uncle Luis talk about the mysterious ways of women. "They need to be appeased," Luis would say, implying that women were strange creatures impossible to satisfy. His Uncle Luis was his mother's younger brother and had a job at a plant nursery in Albuquerque. He'd been in trouble with the law a few times and had a bitter philosophical outlook on life. Ray didn't know what his uncle meant about women but he believed they weren't to be trusted.

Ray's habit was to run on the dirt road parallel to the highway that went through town. People waved at him or called out to him as he jogged past their properties. He wasn't inclined to wave back. His body seemed out of control and running gave him some relief. He found that it cleared his head and helped him to sleep better. He wore his work shoes to run at first but soon learned that he got blisters. He used the money his grandfather gave him for working during the summer and he bought a cheap pair of athletic shoes that were more comfortable. Ray ran about a mile, then walked, and eventually he came to a small adobe shed that had been in ruins for as long as he could remember. There was no interest in old ruins from anyone in town so no one ever spent the time cleaning them up. They just crumbled away and disappeared into the ground over time. Ray hid some magazines there a while back with the expectation that no one would ever come across them, not even by accident. He moved pieces of tin that fell down from the roof and pulled out a shallow cardboard box that once contained his running shoes. Inside were a couple of *Hustler* magazines. He stomped on some clods of adobe and made a place to sit with his back against the wall.

The first page he opened was the centerfold. It was a poster of a nude woman with her head thrown back and her long neck arched, pale and delicate. Her legs were spread apart in such a way that she seemed to be inviting Ray to put his hand between her thighs. He imagined his hands moving toward the round breasts and the dark triangle below. He thought about long-legged girls from school, their hips swaying as they walked down the corridors past where the boys were squatting at the lockers pretending to be searching for something. All the while they were hoping to get a look under the girls' skirts. He leaned back comfortably, unzipped his pants and began fondling himself. He imagined how it would be with such a woman– to touch her, to taste her skin, her mouth, her privates. He looked at the photo again, at the long curved neck and the sensuous mouth that was partly open as if ready to exhale.

Slowly a strong urge came over him. It was a confusing, angry feeling, an anxiousness that was more than arousal. The feeling was a compulsive urge, a tension that compelled resolution. He closed his eyes and began stroking himself vigorously. The act distracted him and separated him from his feelings. His mind went blank as he stroked himself and focused only on the tumescence in his hand. He worked harder but there was no release. Eventually, he stopped as he realized that he'd rubbed himself raw. He fought the urge to throw up as a wave of nausea overwhelmed him. He whimpered and carefully pulled up his shorts and zipped his pants. The injury, however, was not as overwhelming as his frustration. There was a lump in his throat that made him swallow over and over, but it wouldn't clear. He became agitated, realizing there was nothing to be done and he wanted only to leave. He tossed the magazine into the box, put the lid on, and pushed the box back into the depression beneath the tin. He stood up, pulled the tin over the area, including the spot where he'd had been sitting, looked around and left.

8.

VIOLA WAS DISAPPOINTED that Ray did not help her. She managed to retrieve the tub herself and set it up beneath the wringer of the Maytag. She filled it with cold water from the sink and proceeded to do the laundry. When she filled the basket with freshly laundered clothes, she lifted it and carried it out to the line. She set the basket on the ground and stood up straight to stretch her back. It was the snap she heard almost before she felt it– the sense of something inside her tearing away, feeling suddenly heavy, and the warm flow of liquid streaming down her legs that took her to her knees. She knew Ray had gone back to the University and Rosa was still in school, so she called out as loudly as she could for anyone nearby to help.

The school day ended early for Rosa–she simply left. She was bored with the lecture and caught a ride home with one of the parents there to pick up a sick child. The father of the child asked where she was going and she told him that her mother needed her at home. He didn't question her and gave her a ride as far as the turn-off to her house. She heard her mother's voice calling out as she rounded the corner.

Rosa ran to her and immediately knew what was happening. She went into the house and called Dr. Esquibel's office then grabbed a blanket off the bed and ran outside to where her mother sat. She helped her lie down and put the blanket over her to keep her warm. She stayed by her side until help arrived.

"Mama," she said, her voice trembling. "Don't die, Mama! I called the doctor. You'll be okay," she sobbed.

Viola looked at her daughter and attempted a reassuring smile. She was weak and had lost blood. She already knew that the baby she carried would not survive this. She prayed softly and held Rosa's hand tightly.

By the time Dr. Esquibel arrived, Viola was barely conscious. He made a call and, in what seemed an eternity to Rosa, an ambulance arrived and took her mother to the hospital. Rosa was shaken by the experience and prayed that her mother would recover.

Viola was suffering not only from the illness caused by losing the pregnancy, but she was also depressed over the fact that Dr. Esquibel wanted to talk with her. She wondered if he had observed something that she had not wanted anyone to know. She lay in the bed, propped up in a semi-sitting position, worrying about what he might have to tell her.

Dr. Esquibel entered Viola's room quietly and pulled up a chair close to her bed.

"How are you feeling today, Viola?" he asked her.

"Okay, doctor," she responded, without looking directly at him. Her voice was weak and tentative.

"Viola," the doctor began. "Tell me what happened." He had a serious but solicitous tone in his voice. "Start from the beginning, before you ended up on the ground."

Viola looked down at her hands clasped together on her lap.

"I was doing laundry," she began. "I always do laundry at the end of the week. I had everything done and the basket was full of clothes, so I picked it up and carried it outside to the clothes line. I got a pain when I set the basket down so I stood up to stretch and felt something snap," she paused for a moment then continued. "That was when I felt the pain."

"Viola," said the doctor. "Have you been taking any medications besides the vitamins I prescribed?"

"No, doctor," she said, suspecting that he had a reason for asking. She didn't want to tell him what she had really been doing. "Why are you asking?"

"Well, when I delivered the child, I noticed that she was blue," said the doctor.

"What do you mean, doctor?" said Viola. "Are you saying the baby was already dead?"

"Not exactly," he said. "The child was not yet well enough developed to live on its own, but the blue color had to do with a lack of oxygen. That didn't happen suddenly," said the doctor with an intense look on his face.

"What are you saying, doctor? What could have happened to her?" Viola said, sounding genuinely concerned.

"To be honest, Viola, I don't really know. I haven't seen anything like this before. What I can tell you is that you will no longer be able to conceive another child."

Viola looked directly at the doctor, her eyes momentarily blank, as she processed the information. It wasn't the worst news she could have heard. After all, she had lost children before, so that fact alone wouldn't have been the most

terrible thing that could have happened. She had Rosa and
Ramón after all. But despite the cruelty of her husband and
her mistreatment at his hands, she had a momentary sense of
regret that she had taken matters into her own hands again
because she could not bear to give José the satisfaction of
knowing that he had gotten her pregnant once more. There
was that part of her that despised his drunken behavior even
more than she valued the life he helped create.

"Viola?" asked the doctor, noticing her silence. "The
reason you can't have any more children is because I had
to remove your uterus. The damage was just too great. Do
you understand?" She turned to the doctor.

"Yes, I understand. I'll be all right. I'm feeling tired now,"
she replied, and pulled the bedcovers up near her chin. The
doctor seemed to take the cue that she wanted to be left alone.

"You're in good hands here," said the doctor. "Get some
rest and you'll be ready to go home in a couple of days."

Doña Virginia made arrangements with the priest to
bury the baby in the church cemetery. The infant was
named Luz, after Viola's sister who had died from
smallpox. It was done expeditiously and Viola was unable
to attend. Viola wanted to tell José what the doctor had
said about not being able to have any more children as a
form of revenge, but she knew that once he knew about it,
she would never again have a moment's peace.

9.

RAY HAD NOT SEEN his mother in more than a month, so he cut a couple of classes and took the bus to Los Lunas. He stopped to visit Rosa first, to get her opinion.

"How's Mama?" Ray asked his sister.

"She's better. She lost the baby," said Rosa.

"I heard," said Ray. "I suppose everyone is blaming me."

"Why would they blame you?" asked Rosa.

"Because I should have been helping her," he said, chewing his lip.

"It was going to happen eventually, losing the baby, I mean," said Rosa.

"What do you mean?" asked Ray.

"The doctor said she had some kind of poisoning that was killing the baby. He said it would have been only a matter of time if the incident hadn't happened."

"Incident?" asked Ray.

"She was hanging clothes on the line when the placenta pulled loose inside her. I guess that was when the baby died."

"Do you think I should go see her?"

"Sure, Ray, go."

"Do you think she'll blame me for what happened?"

"No, no little brother. Mama loves you. If anything, she blames herself. Go see her."

Ray stopped to visit his grandparents after he left Rosa. They were happy to see him and commiserated about his mama's bad luck but there was no indication that they blamed him for anything. It gave him the courage to visit her.

When Ray arrived, his mother was sitting in a chair in the kitchen. She had a wild-eyed look on her face but said nothing.

"Mama?" said Ray softly. "Mama, how are you feeling?

His mother looked at him and held his eyes for a few seconds, then looked away toward the window.

"Just look at my flowers, Ray. Aren't they beautiful?"

"Yes, Mama, they are," he replied. Silence.

"Ray, how's school, hijo?" she asked without looking at him.

"It's fine, Mama, fine," he said. Again, silence.

"Have you been to visit Rosa?"

"Yes, Mama. I just came from there."

"She's a good girl," his mother said.

"She is," said Ray. More silence.

He had not seen his mother since the morning of the incident and he recalled their conversation as he left her that day. Ray understood why his mother was avoiding a conversation with him. She was angry with him but not because she lost the baby. She was angry that he had disobeyed her, had confirmed her opinion about men, and she was disappointed with him for proving her right.

Ray met Marcela Corral just after his freshman year. She was auditing his accounting class. A petite girl with dark blue-black long hair and a compact little figure a bit on the heavy side, she had a lovely fresh-looking face with pink cheeks and sparkling, nearly black eyes. Ray noticed her as she arrived late for Wednesday morning class. She sat in the row just behind him and he waited for an opportunity to get her attention. When the professor arrived, everyone settled down to the lesson and Ray forgot all about Marcela. She, on the other hand, had not noticed Ray at all. When class was over, he got up and turned around to say something to her but she'd already gone. He looked around as he left but didn't see her. He hung his head and kicked at the gravel as he walked to his next class.

As luck would have it, Ray had a second chance to talk to Marcela. She was waiting for a friend near the door of the statistics classroom. He hung back a bit to pick the right time to talk with her and saw his chance when the crowd of students thinned out.

"I guess we have the same schedule," commented Ray.

"Do we?" she asked, not paying him much attention.

"Weren't you just in the accounting class?"

"I'm just auditing," she said.

Ray thought that the conversation was going well—at least she was talking to him.

"You're kind of young to be in college, aren't you?" she asked.

"What's too young?" Ray replied.

"Too young to go to parties; too young to go drinking; too young for anything fun," she needled.

Ray looked at her full mouth, glossy with red lipstick. He remembered what his Uncle Luis said about women being strange creatures impossible to satisfy.

A friend arrived and Marcela walked away to join her. Ray stood looking after them for a few seconds then went inside the classroom.

Ray decided that there wasn't much use in trying to pursue Marcela. He didn't like her, exactly, but he was interested in her and didn't quite know why. He saw her around the campus a few times but made no attempt at further contact.

10.

ROSA DID WELL IN SCHOOL but her high school years were something of a blur. She spent more time skipping classes and flirting with boys than she did in serious study. When she turned sixteen she dropped out of high school and had no interest in going to college. She was restless and eager to be on her own. She began to help at her father's tienda several days a week and he was content to leave her there alone. She was good with money and the customers liked her. Rosa liked it because it gave her the opportunity to meet men.

A week after Rosa began working at the store, she met Benny. Benny was a shy redneck in his early twenties who moved from West Texas to Los Lunas for the work. He delivered supplies to the surrounding areas from a distribution center in Albuquerque. The tienda was one of his stops. Rosa liked him and took special pleasure in knowing that she made him nervous. She learned his schedule and was always at the store when he arrived. She planned to get better acquainted with Benny on his next delivery.

Benny arrived on schedule the following week and nervously smiled at Rosa as he entered the store. He didn't quite know what to think of her. He proceeded to haul several sacks of grain, flour and sugar to the storage room.

Upon his return from his third trip to the back room, Rosa blocked his way in the narrow passage between the counters. He couldn't get past her unless he jumped over the counter.

"Come on, Rosie. I ain't got time to fool around with you today. I'm on a tight delivery schedule," he said and pushed back from her. She moved in closer, put her hands on his chest and began fingering inside the spaces between the buttons on his shirt.

"Cut it out," he said without conviction as his voice waivered. He ran his fingers over his head a few times in nervous agitation.

"Come on, Benny. How about a little kiss? I'll let you touch my breasts," she said, insinuating herself against his body.

So intent was she on the seduction and he trying to evade her that neither of them heard the opening and closing of the screen door at the front of the store.

"Rosie?" asked one of a pair of children who had entered. The girl could barely reach the counter as her eyes peered over the top at the couple on the other side. More annoyed than surprised, Rosa turned around, keeping her backside in close contact with Benny.

"What do you kids want?" she asked.

"We want some ice cream," said the other girl.

"I've told you, we don't have ice cream here. You have to go over to Vince's place."

"Then can we stay here and play on the sacks?" asked Angela, the older of the two.

"Not today. I'm busy."

"What are you doing?" asked Tillie, the younger child who was bobbing up and down to try to see over the counter.

"This man just made a delivery and I have to…" She paused, then turned suddenly and said, "Benny, give these girls a quarter so they can go buy some ice cream."

Benny fished in his pants pocket and pulled out some change. He handed the coins to the taller girl.

"Thanks, Benny," they squealed in unison and started skipping toward the door, letting it slam behind them as they went.

Rosa turned back to face Benny, but in the effort to get rid of the children, he managed to extricate himself from behind the counter.

"I've really gotta go, Rosa," he said eyeing the door.

She quickly put her arms around his neck and pushed her bosom tightly against his chest.

"Come on, Benny," she urged. He grabbed her hands and pulled them off of him.

"Gotta go, gotta go," he said nervously. He rushed past her and out the door. She heard the truck start and the tires squeal as he drove away.

She stared after him for a few seconds, shook her head and laughed. She knew it would only be a matter of time before Benny gave in. She could be patient.

⌒⊙≈≋≈⊙⌒

Rosa loved for men to come to the store. They flirted with her and especially liked to hear her laugh. She

DOLORES BORREGO JACOBS

cultivated a sort of helplessness that they found irresistible. She had a way of moving in close to a man where he could smell her cologne and she would say something provocative that aroused him. She was artful and there was a deliberate intelligence about her. She was, after all, her father's daughter.

One afternoon, her Uncle Luis showed up at the tienda hoping to find José. He found Rosa alone in the store and was pleased to see her.

"Rosa de Castilla," he said to her. "How are you doing, beautiful Rosa?"

He grabbed her and gave her a tight hug. Rosa usually would have enjoyed that but her Uncle Luis made her a little nervous. He was good looking but had a slightly feral appearance that put her on edge.

"Tío," she said. "¿Cómo estas? Haven't seen you in a long time? Everything good?" She asked as she backed out of the embrace.

"¿Cómo que no? I've got this job in Burque that keeps me pretty busy." His smile didn't quite match the look in his eyes. "Where's your mama? I heard she was sick."

"Yes, she lost a baby," said Rosa. "But she's feeling better now. She's at the house, I think."

"I'll go see her," said Luis. "After all, I am her little brother," he said and winked at Rosa. "Hey, I've got a little something for my Rosa de Castilla." He put his hand into his jeans pocket and pulled out a thin gold chain with a tiny owl on it. The owl had yellow crystals for its eyes.

"For you," he said, smiling as he watched her reaction.

Rosa didn't know what to make of the gesture, but she appreciated her uncle's gift.

"Thank you, Tío," she said not knowing how to respond. "It's very pretty."

"You wear this, now. Don't hurt your tío's feelings," he said, sensing her reluctance to accept the gift.

"You're a good girl," he continued, "and only good girls deserve to wear beautiful things."

He put the chain in her hand and closed her fingers over it, squeezing her hand tightly to show affection.

"Mama is at the house. She'll be happy to see you, Tío," said Rosa.

Her uncle winked at her again and swaggered out of the store.

When the tienda closed for the day, Rosa went home. She hung the owl pendant from a plastic earring tree that a high-school friend had given her for her birthday. She looked at it a bit longer and thought back to her earliest memory of her Uncle Luis.

She was about ten years old and her uncle had been working for some ranchers cutting and baling alfalfa. He had asked José if he would be willing to coordinate the matanza, an event that involved slaughtering some hogs to feed the ranch hands and their families. Rosa's father had agreed and the animals were delivered a week before the three-day affair was to begin.

Rosa recalled going to the pig pen behind the tienda where the huge white hogs were kept. There were three of them. She and Ray watched their pink flat snouts flex their way around and through the fence rails, sniffing for anything that could be eaten. She and Ray were cautioned not to get their hands too close to the animals, and had been admonished with a story about how hogs had been known to eat people. Rosa, however, liked the way their ears flicked and their tails curled up, so as a challenge she stared down one of the animals who seemed to be watching her with some interest. The hogs provided no end of entertainment for a couple of days, so she went back out on the morning of the preparations.

At first she found the activities interesting as the men filled a fifty-gallon drum with water and started a fire under it to get it boiling. Her Uncle Luis had rolled up the short sleeves of his white T-shirt and was flexing his muscles trying to move a large trough closer to where the drum was heating up. Everything she saw made her curious, so she hung around a while to observe.

Some knives had been set out on a wooden table and among them she recognized the sharp-edged lids from sardine cans and wondered what they were for. Her question was answered as her uncle carefully touched the sharp edge of a lid with his thumb then held the thin metal at a forty-five degree angle to his arm, shaving some of his dark hair. She had a little crush on Luis in those days mainly because he was good looking, but also because he paid attention to her and called her by her namesake, the Mexican actress *and singer, Rosa de Castilla. Even at her young age, she thought that Luis was edgy and restless and always in a hurry to go somewhere else.*

About mid-morning the water began steaming up from the barrel and her uncle went to the pig pen, followed by her father carrying a sledge hammer. Two other men that Rosa didn't recognize followed behind, pulling a sled-like platform. Luis jumped into the pen with the pigs and the pen erupted in chaos. The hogs ran in circles, squealing and grunting and bumping into one another. Luis pushed one over and straddled it, bringing his knee down hard on the side of its huge head. Rosa saw her father jump over the rail into the pen holding the sledge hammer and suddenly realized what was coming next.

She turned and ran, making it half way to the house before she heard a sound unlike any she had ever heard before. It was loud and high pitched with a disturbingly human quality. A hard thud put an end to it but the other animals continued their panicked chorus. She ran into the house straight to her bedroom and closed the door. She lay on the bed and covered her ears with the pillow, trying to focus on anything that would distract her from the terrible sounds she was hearing. Eventually the sounds stopped, but she was upset and not eager to go back out there again.

As Rosa stared at the little owl, she wondered about Luis. He had always been nice to her but since he had gotten out of prison, he seemed different somehow. She had heard that prison changed people, but she had little to go on about what those changes were or how they actually came about. She took the owl chain off the earring tree and slipped it out of sight into the top drawer of her dresser.

11.

MIGUEL ROMERO HAD SEEN ROSA at the store a few times but did not talk to her because her father was there. Sometime later he encountered her at a *quinceanera*, the coming-of-age celebration for his fifteen-year-old cousin. The festivities gave Miguel the opportunity to observe Rosa's fine hour-glass figure and graceful movements. He worked up his courage to ask her to dance a corrida, a traditional Mexican dance that delighted couples with its polka-like tempo. She was light on her feet and he liked her energy and flirtatious behavior so much that he worked up the nerve to ask her to go out with him. She accepted his first offer to go for a ride in his truck and then his next invitation to go to a matinee in Albuquerque. After that, they were seen together so often people assumed they would get married. José, however, was not happy about their dating. Rosa had to sneak out to be with Miguel to avoid any interference or punishment from her father.

For decades, the New Mexico State Fair was scheduled during two weeks in September and was the one event everyone attended. It had something for everyone, old and young alike. The events and exhibits were like any other state fair, with its share of 4-H prize-winning sheep, hogs, chickens, rabbits and yearling calves. The obligatory popcorn, cotton candy, and sugary ice pops together with the redolence of farm animals assailed the senses as soon as one entered the grounds. But the smell of green chile roasting, hamburgers on the grill, and deep-fried churros with sugar and cinnamon were uniquely New Mexican. There was also entertainment in the pavilion where a couple could dance for hours to Al Hurricane Jr. or Los Lobos from East L.A.

And then there was the Midway. It was a place to meet friends or perhaps avoid them. It was a place where you could see or be seen as you wished. The Ferris wheel, the Hammer, the tea cups and the kiddie rides all played music that added to the din of screamers on the rides and the barkers daring people to toss a ping-pong ball into a shot glass for a chance to win a Teddy bear or a unicorn. The favorite place was the House of Horrors. It was the perfect date destination. The girls got extra clingy inside the dark labyrinth and made it easy for a guy to steal a kiss or cop a feel.

Miguel called on Rosa to take her to the Fair. He wore his best jeans, clean cowboy boots, and sported a white western hat like the one worn by Ronald Reagan. In fact, Miguel looked a lot like President Reagan, only shorter. He had slicked-back hair and an easy smile that charmed the ladies young and old alike. He liked being with Rosa because she attracted attention with her laughter and sensuous good looks. She was friendly and knew how to handle herself around his friends. It made other men wish they could be with her. Miguel liked the idea of being the one to possess her.

Rosa, on the other hand, had to sneak out of the house on the pretext that she was going to the movies with some friends. Under no circumstances did she want her father to spoil her date. Luckily, José was not at home when Miguel arrived that afternoon.

"Hey, Chava," he said, greeting her with a quick tug on the brim of his hat. "Looking good!"

Rosa smiled nervously and stepped out the door to join him in his truck. Acting the gentleman, he held the door for her and waited until she had gathered up her skirt before closing it. He climbed into the driver's side and started the truck, all the while looking at Rosa's dress.

"That's a nice dress," he said. "New?"

Rosa nodded. It was pale green with tiny matching buttons all the way down the front. It made her hazel eyes look brighter. A thin belt emphasized her slender waist. Her dark, curly hair was freshly washed but had apparently resisted any effort to style it.

Miguel pulled out of the yard and headed for the highway. About five miles outside of town, Rosa scooted over to sit next to him. He smiled approvingly and stepped on the gas.

When they arrived at the Midway, Miguel ran into several men he knew. Roberto Gurule, his brother Tomás and their friend Isadore Valenzuela were from up north. Miguel had met them before in a card game at Silva's

Saloon along the old Route 66 in Bernalillo. He stopped to talk briefly, but they kept eyeing Rosa.

"Where did you find this wisa?" asked Roberto.

"Look out, hombres," said Miguel attempting humor. "I don't want to have to beat you up for getting fresh with my girl."

"We're just appreciating the view," said Roberto as he smiled at Rosa. She made eye contact with him.

"Maybe you should go up on the Ferris wheel if the view is what you're looking for," she countered.

Miguel stepped forward in front of Rosa.

"What's the problem?" Tomás snickered. "She made of fine china, or something?"

"Hey, boys, show a little respect," said Miguel. "Rosa is a nice girl."

"How nice can she be if she's with you?" Roberto retorted.

"Listen, cabrón," said Miguel, raising his fists and moving closer to Roberto.

"No, Miguel. Don't start a fight." Rosa swung around to face Miguel. She looked over her shoulder at the men and gave them an icy look. "Let's just go," she said.

Miguel stood his ground a bit longer, but relented and grabbed Rosa's hand. "All right, let's go. He turned his back to the three and tipped his hat as he stepped away. "See you around, g e n t l e m e n," he emphasized. Then he and Rosa moved rapidly to join the flow of the crowd.

They had walked for about ten minutes when a woman appeared seemingly out of nowhere and put her arms around Miguel's neck.

"Hey, baby," she said. "Remember Roxy?"

Rosa moved quickly and pulled Miguel away.

"He's taken," she said.

"How about you, honey? You taken, too?" said Roxy, laughing at the look on Rosa's face.

Rosa held Miguel's hand and looked the woman over. The smell of Patchouli cologne was overpowering. Rosa knew the woman was a streetwalker. Her sparkly blue eye shadow and red lipstick made her look much older than she actually was. She wore a turquoise bra that exposed ample cleavage inside her unbuttoned blouse. Her short shorts were Popsicle orange and her long, stacked-heel boots were black and scuffed. There were multiple chains around her neck and rings on the fingers of both hands. Her stare made Rosa uneasy.

"You're mistaken. I'm not the person you're looking for," said Miguel, looking back and forth from the woman to Rosa. He was nervous because he clearly knew the woman and didn't want to reveal it to Rosa. "You working girls are kinda out of your territory, aren't you?"

Roxy smiled.

"We get a little work around here. Sure I can't interest you in some cotton candy?" she said, sliding her hand down her body.

Rosa stared coldly at the woman then turned to Miguel with her hands on her hips.

"Are we here to see the Fair or what?" she said impatiently.

Miguel shrugged.

"You heard the lady. We're here to see the Fair." He tipped his hat once again, and turned sharply on the heel of his boot. Ceremoniously putting his hand through the crook of Rosa's arm, they proceeded down the Midway.

They walked from one end of the Midway to the other before realizing that they had not eaten anything or ridden anything and the time was getting late. They hadn't planned to stay until after dark for fear that Rosa would be in trouble when she got home. Miguel stepped up to a nearby hamburger stand and ordered two cheeseburgers, fries and Pepsis. The food was handed to him in a white paper bag that was too hot to hold. Rosa took it by the rolled up top. Miguel grabbed the drinks and some napkins from the dispenser on the window ledge and led the way to the eating area at one side of the stand.

"I'm starving, aren't you?" said Miguel, looking at Rosa's face. She wasn't happy. Miguel pulled open the tabs on the Pepsi cans and handed one to Rosa.

Rosa was sitting gingerly on the streaked and cracked folding chair, careful not to ruin her dress. Her hands were resting in her lap and she was looking out toward the Midway.

"Come on, Rosie," pleaded Miguel. "Let's eat this food before it gets cold."

"I'm not hungry. You eat it."

"Those people are not my friends. I only met them once, honest."

"How about her?" Rosa asked accusingly.

"R-r-o . . . you mean that girl? I swear, I thought she worked at the bank," said Miguel feebly.

Rosa exhaled sharply through her nose and shook her head.

"You have an explanation for everything, don't you?"

"Come on, Rosie. Have a French fry while they're still hot."

Rosa poked her nose down near the open bag and relented when she smelled the warm potatoes sprinkled with salt.

"I'll have a couple," she said, shrugging her shoulders. "Where's the ketchup?"

"¡Ay! I forgot it—just a minute." He pushed himself back on the folding chair. Without warning, the chair gave way and he and the chair fell backwards, knocking off his hat. He jumped up from where he'd fallen, grabbed the hat and began shaking and thumping the dust off the bottom of the brim where it touched the dirt.

Rosa couldn't help herself. She began to laugh until tears sprang into her eyes. Miguel scowled and muttered some obscenities under his breath as he walked back to the hamburger stand for the ketchup. When he returned, Rosa was still giggling. She pulled a cheeseburger out of the bag and set it on a pile of napkins. She pulled off a piece of the bun and nibbled at it. Miguel plopped the ketchup packets onto the table, picked up the fallen chair and sat more carefully this time. He looked up at her with a sheepish grin on his face and put the hat back on his head a little sideways.

"I think it looks better that way," she teased. She took a packet of ketchup, tore it open and squeezed it over a few fries.

Unknown to most Fair goers, there was a darker side to the Fair that went virtually unobserved. It was a web of illicit activity among prostitutes and drug dealers who relied on the anonymity of ever-moving crowds of people and the deafening contrapuntal din of mechanical motion and music to cover their activities. Anyone could be a criminal and the news never lacked a report about a missing child or a break-in at the parking lot. During the two weeks of the Fair, prostitutes did more business than any single month at their regular places. Not surprisingly, drunkenness and disorderly conduct kept the security guards busy from morning to night. The only saving grace, if it could be called that, was the fact that there were only two places to legally enter and leave the fair grounds. Yet it never seemed to present an obstacle to anyone with a more personal agenda.

A few yards from the entrance to the Midway was the concession set-up for easy access to deliveries from outside the grounds. The back area was partially hidden from view due to the unsightly containers of propane, refrigeration units and boxes of packaged and canned food, all crisscrossed by power cords, plumbing and tubing that made everything go. A person could stay there unnoticed for hours, as long as the front side was working smoothly, so it was not a surprise that the prostitutes and their clients found their way back there for some quick relief.

One young woman was convinced by the generosity of her guest to leave the grounds and find a more suitable location for their activity. They left arm in arm and went straight to the parking lot. The man politely held the door for her as she got into the car. He drove southwest, telling her that he was going to take her to the Isleta Casino. She could have all the money she wanted to play and whatever she won was hers. She was excited about her luck. Twenty minutes into the trip, he pulled over at a rest stop, saying he had to pee. He told her to get into the back seat and wait for him. He wanted a little foreplay. She did as she was asked.

Her body was one of those found on the West Mesa.

12.

RAY TOOK A BREAK from studying and decided to go to the Fair for a few hours. He normally didn't like crowded places but for old times' sake he wanted to ride the new roller coaster featured that year. He caught the bus from campus and was at the gate to the Midway in less than thirty minutes. He made his way along the outside of the throng of rides, vendors and visitors and cut across the Midway to the roller coaster. The line was not long when he arrived and he got into a car and secured the bar.

As the cars moved along the track to accommodate more passengers, Ray's car began climbing and he could see more of the Midway below. He looked around to take in the view and spotted someone wearing a white Ronald Reagan hat moving with the crowd. He recognized Miguel and Rosa immediately. He watched them with curiosity. They seemed to be in a big hurry. A woman from the crowd stopped to talk to them. She seemed to know Miguel, but in a moment the pair was walking again. He watched them until the roller coaster started its nonstop mechanical climb and he lost sight of the hat.

When his car reached the top of the structure, Ray held his breath out of habit. He'd been to previous fairs and ridden all the vomit-inducing rides that were available, but he particularly liked this year's new roller coaster because it had two sharp drops that made him feel weightless and euphoric. He rode it twice and on the third time, he looked across the Midway and spotted someone he was sure was his Uncle Luis hugging one of the women who were hanging around not far from the pavilion. His uncle was feeling her sides with his hands and leaning into her, obviously saying something to her. She appeared to resist, but his uncle grabbed her by the arm and started to pull her along, turning his head and pointing with his chin in the direction of the exit. She seemed reluctant to go with him but he was insistent. Ray lost sight of them as the coaster cars started their fall.

This was not Ray's first visit to the Fair and he knew his way around the grounds. He deliberately walked by a couple of gaudily dressed women who offered him a better ride than any he'd had so far. Ray checked them out and went on his way. He went over to a hot dog stand and ordered one with everything on it. He was handed a cardboard tray with a hot dog in a bun overflowing with onions and relish. He munched on it as he walked. He wasn't in a hurry but was curious about the women so he went back to check them out.

The two women were joined by a third and she was arguing with them about something. They kept looking around to see who was watching. The argumentative woman held out her hand and one of the others handed her a thin roll of bills. The three separated and went off in different directions. One of the women bumped into Ray who was leaning against the trunk of an elm tree trying to stay out of the sun. He smiled at her and she smiled back, coyly slipping something into her purse.

"You all by yourself?" she asked beginning her proposition.

Ray nodded.

"Want to have a little fun?" She ran her finger from the center of his chest down to his belt.

Ray shrugged and ate the last bite of his hotdog.

The woman smirked as she watched him.

"How old are you, anyway?" She asked.

"Old enough," he replied.

"A man of few words," she teased. "Well, man of few words, how about joining me for a cool drink inside the pavilion. It's friggin' hot out here."

"Okay," said Ray. "You buying?" He repressed a smile.

"Listen to you getting all sassy. Am I buying? Honey, I don't give nothin' away for free."

She looped her finger through a silver chain that held a two-inch cross, the kind with a little glass dome in the center that magnified the Lord's Prayer inside. He pondered the disconnection between the woman's profession and the religious symbol she wore.

"What exactly are you giving?" asked Ray.

"Why, conversation, of course. I'm thinking you might graduate from two words to a whole sentence after you've gotten out of the sun and had an RC. How about it?"

"All right," Ray agreed. He was thinking that he had at least an hour before he had to catch the bus back to campus.

They walked into the pavilion where there was open space for events and some tables and chairs set up for visitors who might need to get out of the sun. On one end was the concession where soft drinks were dispensed. Ray pulled out a couple of dollars and some change from his pocket and ordered two RC colas. They found a table off to one side and sat down.

"Come on, now," said the woman. "I'll bet you're a student."

Ray said nothing.

"Let me guess. Science major," she said.

Ray smirked.

"That's it, isn't it? Physics or chemistry? Tell Nadine all about your plans, honey."

Ray stared at her pleasantly.

"You remind me of somebody," she said.

"Sure," said Ray. "Occupational hazard, I'm sure."

"Wise ass, aren't you, man of few words. What's your name?"

"Friends call me Ray," he said.

"So now we're friends," she said, pretending surprise.

"I guess we are today," said Ray.

"Hey, I like that," said Nadine.

"Can I ask you a question?" Ray said.

"Sure, honey. What's on your mind?" She leaned forward to give him her full attention.

"I saw you and the other girls arguing with a guy earlier today. Who is he?" asked Ray, not wanting to give away too much at once.

"Listen, honey. Our business is guys, and girls, whatever turns you on."

"No, no," said Ray. "I'm talking about the guy near the end of the Midway who was arguing with you and then left with the other girl."

"You mean Chulo? We don't know his real name. We call him that because he treats us all like dogs," she said with obvious disgust.

"What do you mean?" asked Ray.

"He's always coming by to get money or sex and never pays us back for anything. We think he's bad news but we can't seem to avoid him."

"Hm," said Ray. "Is that all you know about him?"

"One of the girls thinks he's a gardener. He wears work shoes that are always covered with dirt."

"I see," said Ray and grew silent again. He looked at his watch. "I've got to catch the bus," he said. "I've got to go."

"Okay," said Nadine. Don't take any wooden nickels, man of few words named Ray."

Ray laughed.

"See you around, Lady of the Midway named Nadine," he replied and took off in a slow jog toward the exit. She waved at his back.

13.

THE SUN HAD NEARLY SET when Rosa and Miguel returned from the Fair. He stopped the truck within view of the house but not close enough to be noticed. Rosa saw her father's truck parked in the yard.

"Let me off here," she said anxiously.

"I'll walk you up to the door," he replied. "I'm not afraid of your dad."

"No, I don't want any scenes tonight," she said as she opened the passenger door. Miguel caught her hand before she could get out.

"How about a little goodnight kiss?" he said. She repressed the urge to giggle.

"Not tonight. Let go, Miguel. It's getting dark," she said anxiously as she pulled her hand away.

"Have it your way. I'll see you tomorrow," he told her.

Rosa ran around the back of the house to the window of her bedroom. She had left the window open about a half inch just in case. Quietly, she raised the window and slipped inside her room, then she lowered it part of the way. She tiptoed toward the doorway and stood listening for any indication that her father might be nearby. She knew her mother had gone to stay with a sick aunt for a couple of days, so she was relieved when she heard nothing. She groped her way toward the night stand to the right of her bed intending to turn on the light.

"Where have you been, Rosa?" said her father in a belligerent voice. He was sitting in the darkness in the corner of her room.

Rosa drew in a sharp breath and uttered a small scream, as she realized that her father had been waiting for her.

"We went to the movies, Papá. The girls wanted to see…" She didn't finish.

"You're lying," said José as he stood up and came towards her.

"You went out with that *sinverguenza*. He has no shame. Are you trying to make a fool of me?"

"I didn't, Papá," she insisted. "I'm not." She could tell by his voice that he'd been drinking.

Her father moved closer and slapped her hard across the face. She lost her balance and landed backwards on her bed. He stood over her as she lay stunned by the blow.

"I'll teach you to lie to me," he threatened. He crawled onto the bed and straddled her. His fist came down hard against the side of her head.

"You will never lie to me again," he said, and struck her a second time.

"Never!" he said and his fist came down again.

Rosa muffled her screams and put her arms across her face. Her father was furious and out of control as he grabbed her by the hair and rained blow after blow on her arms and head. She whimpered with each blow and became resigned that no one would come to her rescue. She tried to move her body into a fetal position for more protection, but her body was trapped beneath him on the soft mattress.

Abruptly the blows stopped. She lay whimpering with her eyes squeezed tight and her head sheltered under her arms waiting for the blows to resume. Her head hurt and she wondered if any bones had been broken. Her father was breathing hard but said nothing for what seemed like a long time. Suddenly she felt a rough, groping hand reach under her dress and pull down her panties. She peeked out and saw that her father had lowered his pants and was beginning to drop himself on her.

"No, Papá, please, no!" she cried and struggled, putting out her hands to push him off. He was beyond her pleading influence.

The smells of his acrid sweat and raw liquor were nauseating. He pushed her arms down onto the bed to immobilize her and then forced her legs apart with his knee. Her eyes were closed tight and she couldn't move. A sound began to emanate from somewhere deep in her chest as he forced himself on her, but the sound stuck in her throat and couldn't escape. She felt something break inside her and the pain took her breath away.

When her father was spent he rolled over beside her and fell into a motionless torpor. His stertorous breathing was the only sound she could hear. She lay still for a few minutes trying to understand why this had happened to her. Why had her father done this to her? He was the one who was supposed to keep his daughter safe from such an assault. As the enormity of it overwhelmed her, she put her arm across her eyes and wept. Fear and pain begin to flood her body. Her only thought was to get out. She slowly and quietly rolled over to the edge of the bed, realizing that she was injured in several places. She stood up and slowly pulled her panties up from her ankles. She smoothed her crumpled dress and her tears began to fall again. Her head hurt so badly she couldn't think as she walked toward the kitchen, then out the door and across the yard to her grandparents' house. She arrived there in a daze.

"Rosita!" exclaimed her grandmother. "¿Que te pasó, mijita?"

Rosa couldn't tell her grandmother what her father had done to her. She would never believe him capable of it. Rosa lied to her.

"I fell down and hit my head, Grandma," said Rosa. "Can I stay here for a while?"

"¿Cómo que no? Come in here and let me make the bed in the other room for you," said her grandmother. "Where's your mama?"

"She's staying with Tía for a few days."

"O, sí, sí," said her grandmother, remembering. "Don't worry. I'll take good care of you. Let me get you a towel with some cold water. How did you hit your head?" she asked as she disappeared into another part of the house.

Rosa felt a wave of grief and shame come over her and the tears streamed steadily down her face. She leaned against the door frame, realizing that her shoulder and arm were sore from the beating. She looked at the bed where she and Ray spent many nights as children sleeping at their grandparent's house. A sob caught in her throat as she mourned the innocence of those days. Her head throbbed as she tried to make sense of things.

Her grandmother returned with a small towel and Rosa winced as she pressed the wet, cool cloth against her head. She didn't want to think about anything at that moment. She wondered if aspirin could help. She knew that she would probably be black and blue by the next day. Already she could feel where her head was swollen in places.

"What happened to you, hijita? "Was it that Miguel who hurt you? Tell your grandma."

"No, Grandma," she said. "Miguel wouldn't hurt me. I just fell and hurt my head. I think I'm ready to lie down now," said Rosa.

"Of course, mijita, of course," said her grandmother. "Here is a soft pillow for you." She grabbed a pillow out of the wardrobe and handed it to Rosa. "You sleep now. I'll wake you up in the morning."

When Rosa was finally alone, she lay on the bed like a statue. The slightest movement caused her to feel that the room was spinning. She closed her eyes and put the wet cloth over them, hoping that her throbbing head would stop long enough to let her sleep. As soon as her eyes closed, the memory of her father caused her to tremble. She began to cry again. The traumatic events of the day swept over her in a suffocating cloud of sleepiness and she drifted into unconsciousness.

It was eight o'clock the next evening when Rosa's grandmother checked in on her for the fourth time. She had let her sleep because Rosa seemed peaceful and needed rest, but she had questions for her granddaughter. Rosa was not prepared to answer any more questions and asked her grandmother to let her sleep a little longer. After her grandmother left, she got up from the bed and went to the bathroom. She had felt something break when her father violated her and now she saw the evidence—blood on her panties. Her tears started to fall once more as she sat on the commode thinking about how she would explain that she was no longer a virgin. She felt sorry for herself. Her father had broken more than her hymen. He had also broken her heart.

Rosa suffered a terrible headache after the beating. Her eyes were bloodshot and she looked like she'd been in a car accident. She was afraid to go back home where she would see her father, and she didn't want to face her mother who had returned home that morning.

"Grandma, can I stay with you and Grandpa for a few days?"

"Of course, Mijita. ¿Cómo que no? I'll tell your mama and Papá that you are helping me," volunteered her grandmother.

Rosa's head was pounding as she sat down on the bed. She was afraid to go to sleep, afraid that some irreparable damage had been done to her brain that she wouldn't recover from. She endured the throbbing headache for weeks.

José suffered from alcoholic blackouts and didn't seem to remember what he'd done to his daughter. He couldn't understand why Rosa didn't want to see him. Viola knew nothing of what had happened between him and Rosa and tried to explain it away as growing pains. She told him that Rosa was trying to be independent. She told him she needed time to herself. He didn't understand and felt strangely sentimental about the rejection, but he agreed to give her some time on her own. Viola was relieved that José didn't make an issue of it. She, on the other hand, was very worried about Rosa, so she went to Doña Virginia's to talk with her.

"Rosa!" she said, shocked to see her daughter's bruised face and arms and her bloodshot eyes. "What happened to you, mi hija?"

"I fell, Mama," said Rosa calmly.

Viola took a long look at her. "Did someone do this to you?" she asked suspiciously. "You can tell your mama."

"Like I said, Mama, I fell."

Viola shook her head.

"Your Papá is asking for you. What shall I tell him?" she said, leaning toward her daughter.

"Don't tell him anything," Rosa said quickly. "There's nothing to tell. I'll be staying here with grandma for a while."

Viola didn't know what to make of Rosa's refusal to see her father. She was fully convinced that something was wrong, but she knew her daughter, and further discussion would achieve no purpose, so she acquiesced.

"Bueno," she said. "Tell me when you're ready to go back home."

Viola's heart felt heavy as she left her mother-in-law's house. Something was not right but she couldn't put her finger on it.

Rosa missed her period the following month and wondered if a head injury could affect her cycles. When she started throwing up in the morning, she knew from having observed her mother that morning sickness meant she was probably pregnant. Anxiety took hold of her. She began to consider the consequences. She wanted to run away, to go somewhere where no one knew her. There was no practical way to accomplish that but she was positive that no one could find out about it, especially not her mother. She decided that this was the best time to move into the little casita at the back of her grandparents' property. She counted the benefits of such a move. She could avoid her father and mother. She would have more freedom to come and go as she needed to. Most important of all, it gave her the privacy she needed to conceal herself as her body expanded. She had a little money saved from working at the tienda–it would be enough to buy what she needed until she could find a job somewhere.

A dark thought began to form as a replay of the assault spun through her mind. Nausea rose in her gorge. She ran to the bathroom and leaned over the toilet. She became more certain that the only answer was to get rid of the pregnancy. A child of incest is an abomination, she remembered reading somewhere. She thought about how she could do it without killing herself. An abortion would be impossible. She didn't have enough money and no doctor in town would hear of it. There had to be another way.

Her mind rapidly considered alternatives. If she had the child she would have to give it away because it would be a reminder every moment of her father's savagery. Her family would be angry at her and would insist on knowing whose child it was. Perhaps she could hide until the baby was born and then leave it on the steps of the church. She quickly dismissed that alternative. What if she were married? No one would question how the baby was conceived. She could make Benny think he was the father, she thought. He liked her and she could get him to sleep with her. He had a good job and she could move away with him. She weighed the pros and cons of that plan.

She rejected one idea after another. Not Benny, she thought. It would have to be Miguel. She had to get Miguel to marry her. He would never have to know that the baby was not his. He liked her well enough and now he had a job. She would have to act quickly to avoid suspicion. A month, give or take a couple of weeks, could be explained, but unless the baby was small and fragile at birth, no convincing argument could be made that a full-term baby was born prematurely. She set her plan into motion.

Miguel had told Rosa that he was temporarily moving to Albuquerque to take a job at San Bar Construction, a new company that was forming and hiring labor. She reasoned that she would have to go to him since he was living there to be close to his new job. She hadn't seen him since the State Fair and hoped he hadn't found himself a new girlfriend already.

Rosa waited for Benny the next day as he was leaving the tienda.

"I need a ride into Albuquerque," she told him. "I've got to visit a sick friend. Can you take me?" Benny looked at her bruises, hesitated for a moment, then agreed.

"Don't try anything funny," he warned her. He wanted to ask her about the bruises but decided against it.

"Cross my heart," she said, suppressing the urge to laugh for the first time since the assault.

The ride to Albuquerque was not unpleasant, although Rosa had a lot on her mind. She carried a small satchel suggesting that she planned to stay with her friend for several days. Much to Benny's secret disappointment, she behaved herself. They talked about the scenery and the livestock, how the river meandered and about the Indian dances at Isleta Pueblo. When they reached the city, Rosa asked Benny to drop her off on the South end of Broadway. She stopped at a 7-Eleven to ask for directions to San Bar. She assumed that Miguel would be at work and she headed out, intent on finding him.

14.

ROSA WAS SEVENTEEN WHEN SHE married Miguel Romero. He wanted a large wedding, but Rosa convinced him that they should get married by a Justice of the Peace right away so that her father couldn't stop them. Miguel went along with her because he'd already had experience with her fears about her father.

"I will be Mrs. Miguel Romero," she told him, and he smiled at her proudly.

At first she was relieved that things had gone so well, but she felt like a fraud. Rosa liked Miguel well enough but she was not in love with him. He, on the other hand, was glutted with happiness and bragged to all his friends that he'd been the one to finally get her. They spent the next few days getting acquainted as newlyweds and Miguel didn't seem to notice anything unusual about Rosa when they made love. Only she knew that she wasn't a virgin and was prepared with an answer if Miguel had brought it up. She would blame it on an accident when she was a little girl trying to ride her brother's bicycle. She knew Miguel wouldn't question her about the details, as long as he was satisfied with the quality of their intimacy.

After a few days, however, Rosa complained that she was not feeling well. Her bruises had healed but she continued to suffer from headaches. She feigned an apology to Miguel blaming her illness on homesickness. She had never been away from home like that, she told him, and she missed her family. Miguel was disappointed but he attributed her sadness to a lack of experience with men. She stayed with Miguel in the city for a few more days, then returned to Los Lunas. He wanted to please her and gave her some money, promising to come and visit on weekends.

Rosa was glad to be away from Miguel because she was afraid that he would notice the changes in her body. The idea of getting rid of the pregnancy had not left her. She was hoping that he wouldn't find out that she was pregnant before she could do something about it. She moved into the casita and, soon after, her mother stopped by to bring her some clothes and household items. Rosa told her mother that she and Miguel were married.

"Rosa!" said her mother. "What have you done?"

"I'm sorry, Mama, but I just didn't want you to have to pay for a wedding. Who cares, anyway?"

"I care! Your father cares. We all care! Why would you do such a thing?" said Viola.

"It doesn't matter, Mama," said Rosa. "It's done."

"Where is your husband? Why didn't he come with you?" asked her mother.

"He had to work, Mama. I'll be living here and Miguel will come home on the weekends. We have it worked out," she said.

Viola was hurt and disappointed that Rosa chose to marry the way she did. She had hoped for a big church wedding for her daughter. She knew Rosa was headstrong and had to do things her own way, but she'd had her doubts about Miguel all along. She didn't share them with Rosa for fear that it would cause an argument.

"Well, now that you are a married woman, do you think a visit every now and then from your mama would be acceptable?"

"Of course, Mama," said Rosa and hugged her around the shoulders, being careful not to press her body too close. The hug felt distant and insincere to Viola but she said nothing.

"What shall I tell your father? He's going to be furious!" said Viola.

"Tell him whatever you want, Mama. Just don't tell him to come and see me," said Rosa with a cold expression.

Viola shook her head.

"He's going to get drunk," she said. "You know how he is when he's drunk."

"Then don't tell him. He doesn't have to know that anything is changed," said Rosa.

"He keeps asking me about you. It's only a matter of time before he shows up here," said Viola.

"Mama," said Rosa. "I don't want to see him. There's nothing more to say about it."

Viola didn't understand why Rosa still felt the way she did about José. She couldn't imagine what sort of argument could have led to such a serious break in their relationship. She kept her thoughts to herself but couldn't shake the feeling that something else was seriously wrong.

The following week Viola brought a few items for the casita using her visit as a pretext to see Rosa. The visit allowed her to notice that Rosa was beginning to look pregnant.

"Rosa, you have the look of a madonna, mija. Are you already pregnant?" she asked.

"Yes, I think so, Mama," Rosa said to her mother. "I've only just missed my period."

"Have you told Miguel?"

"I'll tell him this weekend when he comes to see me," said Rosa. She had no intention of telling him anything.

"I can't believe that I am going to be a grandmother," said Viola, her face flushing with happiness. She hugged Rosa again, more closely this time.

Rosa was worried that her mother was too observant. She feared she would become suspicious and not believe that Miguel was the father. That would create an entirely different set of consequences than the ones she'd prepared for. More than anyone, Rosa's mother understood pregnancy and its effects on the body. She watched her mother endure several pregnancies over the years. She grew sicker and sicker during each pregnancy until she eventually lost the babies. She remembered that her mother's friend Guadalupe Gabaldón was a curandera and visited her each week with a special tea to drink, but it didn't seem to help. The babies died anyway. Each time her mother lost a baby she would be sick and stay in bed for a week.

For the first time, it occurred to Rosa that perhaps her mother had not lost her babies by accident. She considered the possibility that her mother had taken matters into her own hands with the help of Guadalupe. The thought, while still vague, presented her with a possible solution. Rosa had overheard many conversations between her mother and Guadalupe discussing the benefits of medicinal herbs. Her mother seemed highly influenced by the woman and on her advice started growing specific plants in her garden. Rosa wished she could consult secretly with Guadalupe now for a special herb to rid her of the pregnancy. But for all her healing wizardry, Guadalupe was no match for a ruptured appendix. It was rumored that Guadalupe had died the week after Rosa's mother lost Luz, and her body was returned to Guadalajara. Rosa became convinced that the answer to her condition was some herb that Guadalupe knew about. She decided to take a closer look at her mother's garden.

Rosa walked across the yard to the side of the house where her mother had the garden. She looked about to see if anyone was around, then broke off several stalks of a few herbs that she didn't readily recognize. She grabbed a handful of fragrant mint stems and returned to the casita. She put the stalks in a pitcher with water, locked up her house and walked to the main road.

The bus made four runs each day: once in the morning so people could get to work, two during the lunch hour and one at the end of the day so people could come home from work. Rosa caught the end of the lunch run and got off at the library. She went directly to the plants section and pulled out several books on herbs. She found one containing pictures of various plants and immediately recognized a plant from her mother's garden. She learned that the plant was comfrey, an edible green with a striking growth habit. She kept reading. Eventually she found an entry for rue, and recognized it as the ruda plant that was nearly taking over one side of her mother's garden. Rue, the book said, was a toxic plant, historically known to aid in menstruation. Rosa knew that this was the plant her mother used for tea and it dawned on her that a plant that could stimulate menstruation might also stimulate an abortion. She looked for other herbs with that property but had no luck. She guessed that Guadalupe must have provided her mother with something additional to put in her tea. Rosa had no way of knowing what that could have been but she was desperate and willing to try the rue.

15.

SEVERAL MONTHS HAD PASSED AND Rosa decided that she couldn't wait any longer to start using the rue. She was glad to see her mother each week but didn't tell her about the rue tea she'd been drinking. She asked her mother to bring her some mint from her garden and added sprigs of the fragrant mint to camouflage the smell and appearance of her cup of tea. Rosa didn't know what to expect but it didn't take long before she began to feel the effects of the herb. Her mother worried about her and believed that she was not handling the pregnancy well. Viola's concern grew and she wanted Rosa to see a doctor. Rosa assured her that it was only a little cold or indigestion and promised to see the doctor soon. She convinced her mother that all she needed was rest. Her mother reluctantly left her alone.

Rosa expected to see her mother on Thursday and had decided to tell her the truth about how she got pregnant, but thought better of it. She couldn't bring herself to hurt her mother with that information. And there was Miguel. She had to keep the whole thing quiet for fear that he would find out, or even worse, that her father would get involved.

Rosa grew more ill and laid in her bed. She wanted to believe that she had flu and her digestive system was rebelling, but she knew it was the effects of the rue. She didn't want to think about the life inside her, but she knew that if she was sick, the child must also be sick. Guilt crept in and she began to doubt her decision. She knew that what she was doing was wrong, but given how the child was conceived, she believed that it would be a greater sin to allow it to live. She wrapped her arms around her middle and cried herself to sleep.

❦

Viola had been asked to launder and iron the linens for the church and planned to work all day on Thursday to get it done, so she went to see Rosa on Wednesday. She showed up at Rosa's casita early in the morning. She knocked and tried the door at the same time, surprised to find it unlocked.

"Rosa?" she called softly.

"Here, mama," said Rosa weakly. She was lying on the bathroom floor in a pool of watery blood. Her voice was weak and her breathing labored.

"Mama," whispered Rosa again. "I think the baby is dead."

Viola was shocked to see her daughter on the floor, but moved quickly into action.

"Lay still, hija," she said. "Let me get some sheets."

Viola went to the bedroom and found two blue sheets in the bureau. She folded one sheet in half and slid it under Rosa, then kneeled beside her and put her ear to Rosa's abdomen before covering her with the other sheet. She got up from the floor and closed the windows, drew the curtains and locked the door. She grabbed a clean pot holder from the kitchen and kneeled beside her daughter.

100

"We'll have to do this by ourselves, Rosa," her mother told her as she turned back the sheet. "You'll have to push the baby out if you can."

"It hurts too much," cried Rosa.

"I'll help you. Let me push down on the top." She rolled up the potholder and put it between Rosa's teeth. "Ready? One, two, three, PUSH!"

Rosa drew her legs up and cried out in a long, muffled groan as she pushed.

"AGAIN!" said her mother.

Rosa had no strength to push.

"Let me take a look at you," said her mother and looked under the sheet to inspect her daughter more closely.

"¡Dios mío!" said Viola. "I can see the baby's feet! I'm sorry, mija. You're right. There's no way this baby can survive coming this way. How many months?" she asked. Rosa held up her hand to indicate five months.

"I'm going to try to pull this child out, Rosa. It is going to hurt. You have to be strong, hija. First, I have to grab the baby's feet with a towel so my hands don't slip. Are you ready?"

Rosa nodded feebly and let out a muffled scream through the potholder. Her insides felt like they were being pulled out.

It was late afternoon. Viola entered the small two-room storage building carrying a small package wrapped in brown paper loosely covered with a burlap sack. She locked the door behind her, grabbed a short Army trenching shovel from the wood box near the stove, then walked directly to the back of the second room where a door used to be. She stood in silent contemplation staring at the large piece of linoleum covering the threshold. She knelt down and set the bundle carefully on the floor to her left, then grasped the edge of the linoleum securely and flung it over to the opposite side. She unwound the gunny sack and spread it over the linoleum. She took up the trenching shovel, pulled up the pick and locked it into place by turning the ring at the throat of the implement. She began digging into the hardened dirt. She prayed as she worked, breaking up the dirt, lifting it out with the spade then carefully dropping it onto the burlap. She murmured rhythmically in a barely audible monotonic voice as she moved the dirt. Her hair hung down in wispy strands and more than once she stretched out her back.

After thirty minutes her face was red and dripping with sweat, and the front of her dress was wet from her throat down and across her bosom. She had carved out a narrow opening roughly one foot by two and about eighteen inches deep just inside the foundation of the building. She set the shovel down on the pile of dirt, wiped her forehead with her sleeve and turned to collect the bundle. She cradled the child gently and talked to its swaddled form.

"*Mi nieta querida*," she said. "My beloved granddaughter, I will never again hold you in my arms and sing you to sleep. You will never know how special a first grandchild is or how my heart aches because we will never know each other. I'm not able to bury you properly in the church cemetery but sleep with God, mi niñita. May God forgive me, for putting you in such a lonely place. I will never know a day of peace for what I do tonight."

Gently, she placed the bundle into the hole, the sound of her prayers growing faster and stronger. She retrieved a small rosary from her apron pocket, laid it on the bundle and ended the informal ceremony with a final sign of the cross over the infant.

She rose and walked around to the far side of the burlap, picked up the two corners and pulled them to the edge of the hole, rolling the dirt inside. She went back to the other side of the grave and, with considerable strength, pulled the top of the burlap toward her so that the dirt rolled neatly into the grave. A small mound formed on the floor. She dropped to her knees and began firmly pressing the dirt down with her palms. She gathered in the small clods of claylike dirt that strayed from the mound and pushed them down firmly until the area was flat and hard. She stopped to catch her breath. With a final effort, she grabbed the board, placed it over the grave and pushed it in until it fit where it was before. She got the broom and swept up the dirt that didn't fit into the grave and placed it in the gunny sack. She replaced the linoleum, eyeing it closely to ensure that her work couldn't be detected. When she was satisfied, she gathered up the burlap and tied the ends into a bag that went over her shoulder. She grabbed the broom and shovel and dropped them both next to the wood box as she walked toward the exit. She opened the door, briefly looked around, straightened her shoulders and walked out of the building.

16.

ONE MORNING RAY was walking across the campus and recognized a student as one of the girls he had seen with Nadine at the Midway. She was on campus taking a nursing class.

"How's your friend Nadine doing?" he asked her.

She seemed startled by his question.

"How do you know her?"

"We shared a drink at the Fair back in September. She's a funny girl," said Ray.

"I guess I can tell you, then," said the girl. "Nadine is gone."

"What do you mean gone? Like moved away?"

"Like, missing," said the girl lowering her voice.

"Missing?" repeated Ray mimicking her softer tone.

"That's right. She left all her stuff at her place and just disappeared. I think something happened to her."

"Like what?"

"Look, I got out of the business because I'm scared that I'm going to end up dead. A bunch of the girls I used to hang with have been disappearing. I had to move away from Central so I could fall off the radar," she said, her eyes wide and furtive.

"It's hard to believe," said Ray shaking his head. "Nadine, huh? If anybody could take care of herself, I thought she could."

"I've said enough. There's a detective who was talking to us about his list. The list turns out to be sixteen women, some he knew, who disappeared from Albuquerque. I know some of the girls on his list." She looked quickly from side to side. "I've really got to go now, or I'll be late for class," she said and walked away in a hurry.

"Good luck," called Ray as he watched her go. Nadine, he thought, shaking his head in disbelief.

Getting his degree gave Ray a strong sense of confidence and his pre-graduation work with clients made it easy for him to slip right into a job as an assessor. He had two cases to work on that summer that kept him busy right away. One involved a fraud investigation at a small credit union. Ray had to conduct a standard audit and he worked with another auditor to prepare the report. The second case was a rancher from the northwest valley in Albuquerque who died unexpectedly and left no will. The rancher's daughter, a recent graduate from the College of Veterinary Medicine at Colorado State University, was living on the ranch and called for an audit of her father's estate. Ray drove across town on a July afternoon to meet with her at the ranch.

"You must be Ray Martinez," she said and extended her hand to him. "You come highly recommended." She had a generous smile and dark blue eyes.

"Glad to hear that," said Ray.

"I'm Catherine, but my friends call me Cate. Let me show you around a bit so you know what you're getting into." Her manner was friendly and welcoming. She led the way to the main house across a grassy field that had recently been mowed.

Ray followed her, trying not to be distracted by her long, shiny, light-brown hair and her well-shaped rear. He had worn his dress shoes, not suited for dodging field stubble and manure, and a business suit, as his job required when meeting with clients. He began to get warm as he walked. He loosened his tie a bit and in a few minutes they had reached the house.

"How about some limeade?" she offered.

"That would taste good about now." He set his leather notebook on the wide wooden arm of a large chair.

Cate disappeared around the corner and left Ray alone to look around. It was a rustic place with a high ceiling made of rough-cut wood rafters; suspended from the central beam was a wagon-wheel chandelier with lanterns all around. The furnishings were heavy and looked like they had been imported straight from the set of the television series, Bonanza. There was a huge stuffed bear in one corner and the mounted head of an elk with eight points per antler hanging over the massive stone fireplace. The room was dark, though the curtains were completely open to let in the afternoon sun. Ray felt a cool breeze waft through the room and was becoming more comfortable.

"Here you go," said Cate as she returned holding a tray loaded with a large pitcher and two glasses filled with iced limeade. She had added slices of lime to the drinks. She set the tray down on the glass table top and motioned to Ray to have a seat.

"I'll have to ask you some questions about your father and the business of the ranch before I can begin the assessment." Ray reached for a glass. He was all business.

"Well, what do you want to know?" asked Cate.

Ray set down his glass and took up his notebook and a pen. He turned to the checklist, scribbled in the date and time and a heading: Martin Ferguson Estate. He looked up at her and began with the first question.

"How much property comprises the bulk of the estate?"

She chewed her lip as she concentrated on the question.

"I heard my father say once that he owned ten thousand acres between his property here and the one in Clovis."

Ray looked up at her.

"How many acres here?"

"Ten," she said without hesitation. "We raise a few Charolais cattle here."

"A few?"

"About twenty head," she estimated. "We bring in their hay."

"Of course, I'll have to get an accurate inventory, but the ballpark figure will work for now." He didn't want to embarrass her by asking for details she couldn't give.

"How many buildings are on this property?"

"Let's see. There's this house, the main barn, the equipment shop, the bunk houses—two of those–and the big barn out in the pasture."

"And the property in Clovis?" he asked

"Nothing out there except antelope and coyotes," she said with a laugh.

Ray liked this interaction. Cate was different from the other women he met at school. She was close to his age and maturity, but she seemed worldly. He suspected that her intelligence and education were the biggest contributing factors, but there was also directness about her that he found attractive. He spent an hour and a half with her discussing the assets of the estate, made another appointment with her for a week later and then excused himself.

Ray drove back to his apartment with his family in Los Lunas on his mind, especially Rosa. He missed her and worried about her; after all, they had grown up side-by-side, inseparable until they started school. His sixth sense told him Rosa was fragile, despite her outwardly assertive behavior. His instinct was to protect her, but from what he didn't clearly know.

17.

VALONDA STEPPED OFF THE GREYHOUND bus at the station on First Street in Albuquerque. She was there by invitation from a friend she knew from her hometown in Chattanooga, Tennessee. She had been surprised that there were no people like her on the bus, but her friend told her there were a few Negro families living in the city. So far she hadn't seen a single individual of her color. She felt alone out in the middle of nowhere and far from her family, but regardless of the circumstances she was better off away from the drug traffic that threatened to swallow her up back home. She had been clean for over a month and although the gnawing need for heroin was always with her, she was feeling stronger than she had in a long time. She'd saved a little money, enough to eat and for bus fare, and her friend Celia had a bed for her at her place on Central.

She went into the bus terminal and used the pay phone. Thirty-five minutes later, Celia pulled up in an old Chevy Malibu, riding next to some guy wearing a fedora.

"Come on, honey. Let's get you situated," she said.

Valonda was relieved to see her and climbed into the back seat without hesitation.

"You had anything to eat, honey?"

She shook her head.

"Here's a bottle of water. This place is drier than a bag of dirt. Let's go get some food, baby," she said to her companion. "This girl must be starved."

The girls were dropped off at Celia's apartment on Central Avenue about a quarter past ten in the evening. The apartment was two bedrooms, a kitchenette and a bathroom. Valonda needed to pee after the long bus ride.

"Here's your bed, honey. You can use the shower but you'll have to get your own shampoo."

"Sure. I got some in ma bag. Celia? Thanks, ya hear?"

"For what?"

"For letting me stay wit ya."

"Don't be silly," said Celia. "You get some rest now. You'll be busy enough tomorrow." She hugged her friend. "Gotta go, now. Duty calls."

Valonda used the bathroom and washed up before crawling into the single bed. She was tired and every time she closed her eyes she saw a dark highway with a white stripe roll out ahead of her. It had been a long trip with many stops at what seemed like every town along the way. She hadn't been able to sleep soundly because she was vigilant about her safety on the bus. When she managed to drift off, the bus stopped to drop off or pick up passengers at every terminal on the route and jolted her awake each time. She felt like a sleepwalker, not awake but not quite asleep either. The bed was a haven. She stretched out full length, touched the wall with her fingertips and pointed her toes almost to the end of the mattress. She reached for the water bottle that Celia had given her and took two long gulps to quench the dry thirst she felt. Eventually, she slept.

The bright sun blasting through the window woke Valonda from a deep sleep. She was a bit disoriented, wondering where she was, but quickly came to her senses as she looked around the little apartment. She noticed a plastic bag on the kitchenette counter. She had slept so soundly that she didn't hear Celia come in. She reached for her bottled water and drank the remainder. She got up and went into the bathroom to get a proper shower. The water took its time getting warm. She wasn't in a hurry, anyway.

"Valonda, honey?" Celia was awake and out of bed. "Can you hurry up in there? I'm about to bust!"

Valonda moved her body under the spray a couple of times to get the soap off, wrapped the towel around her body then stepped out and opened the door.

Celia rushed into the bathroom with only a quick smile as she brushed by.

"Hey, Valonda?" she called from inside.

"Yah, what's goin' on?"

"Can you toss me that box of tampons from the bag on the counter?"

Valonda opened the bag and pulled out a box of hair bleach and a smaller package of tampons. She went to the bathroom door and passed the package to Celia.

"You gonna bleach yo hair today?" she asked.

"No, honey. That stuff is for you. I think you'll get more customers if you lighten your hair a bit. Oh, and before I forget, there's a laundry room down the hall."

Valonda took a better look at the box. It had a picture of a colored woman with reddish blond hair on the cover. She had never tried to color her hair before, although she had gotten pretty good at straightening it. She looked at the instructions. Done in 30 minutes, she read. Hope it don't make ma hair fall out, she thought. Be the shortest career in history for a working girl. She snickered.

After Celia had gone, Valonda wandered down the hall with her sack of clothes to find the laundry room. There was an older woman standing by the dryers waiting for her clothes to dry. Valonda looked askance as her and began feeding quarters into the receptacle on one of the washers. She looked around to see if anyone had left some detergent sitting around but there wasn't any. The woman by the dryers noticed her and introduced herself.

"My name's Gracie," she said. "What's yours, honey?"

"Valonda."

"You must be new in town. You stayin' with somebody here?"

Valonda nodded. "Celia," she responded.

"How old are you, honey?"

"Just turned fifteen," she replied.

"How well do you know Celia?" asked Gracie.

"We's friends from back home."

"Celia must have painted a pretty picture for you about life out here, to make you come so far from home," Gracie continued.

Valonda shrugged. "You got any soap?"

"Sure, honey. Here's just enough for that little bit of washing you got there."

Valonda's first night on the job was nerve-wracking. She stood about twenty feet from Celia along Central and watched the night traffic go back and forth, but no one stopped for her. She couldn't have too many more nights like this before she'd be out of money. Her feet hurt and she could still smell the odor of the hair treatment, despite the generous spray of cologne she had applied. She touched her hair and it felt a bit dry. She noted that she'd have to get some hair dressing at the "open all night" Walgreens a couple of blocks from Celia's. She decided to talk to Celia.

Celia was busily applying a fresh coat of mascara, using a small mirror with a light built into it. She barely acknowledged Valonda as she approached.

"What's going on, honey?" asked Celia without looking up.

"You got any customers tonight?" asked Valonda, even though she already knew the answer.

Celia looked up and shook her head.

"It gets this way sometimes. Don't worry, it'll get better, honey. You go on over there and save your spot, you hear?"

"Sure," said Valonda. "I'm thinkin' I should go to the Walgreens and pick up some pomade for my hair. It's kinda dry."

Celia looked at her for a moment.

"Okay, you go ahead, honey. I'll probably still be here when you get back. Get me an orange Crush, will you?"

"Sure, I'll be back in a bit."

Valonda started walking down the street in the direction of the Walgreens. The street was dark but got brighter as she approached the store. She peered into the window to make sure there were people inside before she entered. She walked around trying to find the hair dressing she needed and then went to where the cold drinks were stored. She noticed a man standing near the coolers, but didn't look at him. She approached the cooler where she saw the orange Crush bottles and pulled open the door. The man moved closer and took hold of the door.

"Here, let me help you with that," he said politely. She looked at him.

"Thanks," she said and grabbed a second bottle for herself.

The man continued to look at her and finally asked what her name was.

"Candy," she said, having been coached by Celia never to give her real name.

"That's a real nice name," he said. "What line of work you in, Candy?"

"Customer service," she said and gave him a wry little smile.

"Well, guess what? I'm in need of some customer service. Can I help you with your things, there?"

"I guess so," Valonda replied, as she handed him the sodas and moved slowly toward the register.

She put the pomade on the counter and he set down the bottles and reached for his wallet. She noticed how he made a show of a wad of bills as he paid the cashier, and figured it was for her benefit.

"Where's your car?"

She looked at him with a crooked smile.

"I'm walking."

"I can't let you do that. That's my truck right back there. I'll take you wherever you want to go."

Valonda's feet were hurting even more after walking the two blocks to the Walgreens and having to walk back to Celia's spot was not an appealing prospect. She hesitated and thought about the offer. She figured she could give him a little customer service for his trouble and maybe she'd see him again. He gathered up her purchase and held the door for her. They walked out together.

The remains of a fifteen-year-old African American woman were later found on the Mesa.

18.

SIX MONTHS LATER, Rosa was still living in the casita and Miguel was working and staying in Albuquerque. Her miscarriage was all but forgotten and Miguel was disappointed that he had no child with Rosa after all this time, but he knew that it would be hard to get Rosa pregnant if he could only see her a couple weekends a month. Rosa, on the other hand, was not one to be lonely. Benny finally gave in to Rosa's demands and was now seeing her once a month when he made deliveries. The two had been trying to keep their relationship a secret, so they were careful. Visits from Miguel had become somewhat unpredictable and he acted suspicious when he came to see her.

Rosa was way ahead of Miguel. She had worked out a system with Benny to let him know when Miguel was home with her. She went to her mother's garden and dug up a well rooted sprout of rosemary and planted it in a pot. She explained to Benny that the Spanish word for Rosemary was *romero*, just like her married name. Whenever he came to see her, he was to check her bedroom window for any sign of the plant on the sill which meant her husband was home, and he should not stop by. This plan worked well for a while until the day that Miguel showed up when Rosa wasn't expecting him.

Miguel came home early one weekend to surprise Rosa because he'd gotten a raise. He had picked up a small television set as a present for her. Rosa, in the meantime, had hurried home to be with Benny when she found Miguel already there with his good news. In her surprise at Miguel's gift and good news, she forgot to put the rosemary plant in the window. Twenty minutes later, when Miguel answered a knock at the door, he found Benny standing there holding a bouquet of flowers.

The two men stared at each other for a second then Benny dropped the flowers and ran.

"What the hell is this, Rosa? You been banging that guy while I'm away?"

"No, no, Miguel," said Rosa. "He's a nice person. I know him from the tienda. He said he'd stop by to cheer me up. I've missed you so much," she said and turned to put her arms around his neck.

Miguel stepped back and rejected her embrace. He knew that she was lying to him.

"I came to tell you about my job, go out to dinner to celebrate or something, but I see that you've found other ways to entertain yourself," he said.

"Come on, Miguel," she chided. "Let's not fight over this silly misunderstanding. Where were you planning to take me?"

He didn't want to be angry at her, so he relented a bit.

"I don't know, Rosa. I don't feel much like going anywhere now except back to Albuquerque. But I'm thinking that when I leave you here alone, you're going to hook up with this guy as soon as I leave the city limits."

"Never," Rosa insisted. "He's nothing to me, honest."

"I'll stay here tonight, but I've got to get back to work in the morning," he said. Rosa was relieved that the argument did not escalate. Miguel fiddled with the television, positioning the rabbit ears antenna to get a better picture. He scraped the antenna contacts with the new Rosewood pocket knife his buddies at the job had given him and cleaned his nails with it as he watched the new TV. He spoke very little to Rosa that night and instead stayed up to watch a movie until he finally went to sleep on the sofa. The next morning he left for work early, still upset.

Back in Albuquerque, Miguel couldn't stop thinking about Rosa and that guy with the flowers. Finally, he convinced himself that Rosa was being unfaithful. He started drinking at night to settle his nerves but his performance on the job began to suffer and he came in late several mornings a week. His co-workers made remarks about his hot wife keeping him up, but their remarks only fueled his suspicions. He was convinced she was sleeping around, so he left work early one afternoon hoping to catch her in the act. He picked up a pint of whiskey and began drinking it as he drove. The liquor made him increasingly angry as he thought about a confrontation with Rosa. He had not been a violent and jealous man, but this business with Rosa had driven him to desperation. He was driving too fast and weaving on the road when he heard the police siren.

"Ah, que chingada," he hissed, slamming his hand against the steering wheel. He pulled his car to a stop on the shoulder of the highway and rolled down the window. The patrolman took his time getting out of the cruiser and walked deliberately over to Miguel's car.

"Sir," he began. "You were weaving on the road and exceeding the speed limit. Have you been drinking, sir?" he asked.

"Aw, hell, officer," he responded. "I found out my wife is messing around and I had a few drinks," said Miguel, feeling even more miserable now than before.

"Where are you headed?" asked the patrolman.

"Los Lunas," said Miguel. "I got to get things patched up with Rosa."

"Rosa? That's your wife's name?"

"Yea, why you asking?" said Miguel suspiciously. "You know her, or something?"

"No sir," was the reply. "Let's see your license and registration."

"Okay," said Miguel and fumbled around reaching in his back pocket for his wallet. He handed the cards to the officer.

"I'll be back in a few minutes," said the officer. He walked back to his vehicle.

Miguel was agitated. He didn't want any trouble with the law. He already had two speeding tickets from driving back and forth from Albuquerque to Los Lunas in his excitement to see his wife, but now he couldn't shake his thoughts about her. He couldn't believe that he was so stupid as to buy what she told him. He thought she was as anxious to see him each week as he was to see her, but now he figured it was all a show. She didn't care anything about him. All she wanted was his money so she could fuck around with other guys while he was working his ass off. The thought made him furious.

The patrolman got out of the cruiser and returned to Miguel's car. He returned his cards.

"I'm going to give you a ticket, sir," said the officer.

"You *chotas* have a very polite way of sticking it up the ass, don't you?" said Miguel.

"You need to simmer down, Mr. Romero or I'm going to have to take you in," said the officer.

"Where you gonna take me *in* to?" asked Miguel sarcastically. "You gonna put me in the slammer?"

"Look, sir. You're too intoxicated to drive. I'm going to have to ask you to step out of the car."

"Hell," said Miguel. "I can walk the line, just watch this." Miguel stepped out of his car and nearly fell down. The officer grabbed him by the arm and led him over to the cruiser and put him in the back seat.

"You arresting me?" yelled Miguel.

"No, sir," said the officer. "I'm going to give you a ride home. Where do you live?"

Miguel was headed to Los Lunas when he was stopped so he told the patrolman that home was there.

"Is anyone at home right now? Your wife?" asked the officer.

"Hey, chota," called Miguel. "Excuse me, officer . . . what's your name? You got a wife?" he slurred his words.

"Name's Zawadzki, Officer Zawadzki," replied the patrolman. "No, not married," he said, wanting to calm Miguel's hostility.

"What kind of a name is Zadsky?" asked Miguel, mispronouncing the name, reacting now rather than thinking. "You a Polack, or something? I bet you're from New York," Miguel persisted.

"Zawadzky," the patrolman corrected him. "Settle down now. Let's get you home. What's your address?"

"I live in Peralta," said Miguel, giving the patrolman the street to his parents' home. "Molina Road."

"You make sure somebody comes to pick up your car tomorrow or it'll be tagged for impound," said the patrolman.

"Sure, sure," said Miguel, now beginning to feel sick. He slumped in the back seat and crossed his arms in resignation. He knew his parents were not home. They had gone to visit his mother's sister in El Paso, but he knew where they kept the spare key.

By the time he arrived at his parents', Miguel was feeling hung over and a little sick. He thanked the officer and walked to the house. He found the key in a small magnetic box stuck to the metal frame beneath the porch swing.

The officer watched him until he was inside the house and then slowly drove away.

They call it 'Hair of the Dog', the remedy for a hangover. Miguel drank down a can of beer with a tequila chaser from his father's liquor cabinet and it fixed him right up. He turned on the TV to pass some time. He decided that a second beer wouldn't hurt and then he had a third, until he was drunker than before. He found the keys to his father truck and headed out the back way to Los Lunas.

He arrived at the casita and found Rosa folding some laundry on the bed.

"How many?" he asked her, barely controlling his voice. "How many have you been screwing while I've been working my ass off?"

She didn't look at him.

"What are you talking about Miguel?" she responded. "What are you thinking?"

"Don't try to deny it," he retorted. "I figured somebody like you would turn out to be a whore. I should have seen it coming."

"What were you talking about, Miguel? Are you still harping about those flowers?"

"Flowers, hell," he tells her. "He was delivering more than flowers, wasn't he? Why don't you just admit it?

He moved a little closer to her and nervously put his hand in and out of his pocket.

"I heard you were kissing him behind the store. You thought no one saw you, but they saw you, *puta*," he said. "Nothing but a whore."

"Who are these people that are accusing me?" she asked. "They're making up gossip." She'd heard this before and was amused at the accusation. "It's just your imagination, Miguel," she said, giggling.

"What the hell are you laughing at? You think this is funny? "

"You have to admit that people are always inventing drama even when there isn't any," said Rosa, sounding like the voice of experience.

"I don't give a fuck about drama," he shouted. "You belong to me, ME!"

Rosa felt a cold tremor make its way up her spine. Miguel was looking at her with an expression she had never seen on his face before.

"One man wasn't enough for you, was it? Come on, Rosa. Show me how you and those guys get it on," he said as he moved towards her.

"Calm down, Miguel," she said, backing away from him.

"Calm down my ass," he said. "You aren't happy unless you're turning some man inside out."

"I'm your wife. Why would I want anyone else?" she tried to reason with him.

"I'll show you what happens to a wife that steps out on her husband. You're gonna do what I say or else!"

She raised her hand and tried to touch him but he caught it and squeezed her fingers. In a flash his other hand came out of his pocket holding the pocket knife. He flipped open the blade with his thumb.

"What? Are you going to cut me?" Rosa asked, angry now, not quite believing he would hurt her. She goaded him. "Go ahead and do it then. Show me how much of a man you are." She eyed the blade.

"You shut your damn mouth. I'll show you something about being a man."

She snorted softly, her disgust with him clearly obvious.

"What do you know about being a man, cobarde?" She called him a coward. "Real men know how to treat a woman. They don't go around accusing them of crimes and making empty threats."

"¡Cabrona, puta!" he said twisting her fingers and holding the blade at the ready.

"Stop it, Miguel. You're hurting me."

In one swift move, he jabbed the sharp blade toward her and the tip of the blade caught her bodice. A red spot began to spread from the tear in her dress. She looked down at the blood rosette forming over her breast and whimpered in surprise. Without hesitating, he lunged at her, striking her again and again, the blade slicing her breasts and arm.

"¡Cabrona, puta!" he yelled as he cut her.

"MAAAMA!" She cried out and fell to the floor covered in blood.

Rosa's terrified screams brought the neighbors out of their homes and establishments to see what direction the sounds came from. Viola heard the screams and came running to see what was happening. People were gathered in the doorway to Rosa's house. Viola pushed her way through the onlookers and burst on the scene. Had it not been for the quick action of one of the neighbors who caught her by the apron straps, Viola would have run directly into Miguel's bloody knife.

"¡Qué chingado!" said one of the spectators. "He's fucked up!"

"He's gone crazy!" Others whispered in shock over what they saw.

Viola found Rosa on the floor and wild-eyed Miguel standing over her. People pressed in to get a better view.

"Put the knife down," they yelled at Miguel.

"Somebody, call the sheriff," said another.

Miguel was backed up against the wall as far as he could, and he realized that all those people had seen what he'd done. He threw down the knife and fled out the back door.

"Move back," cried Viola as she made room around her daughter. "Rosa! ¡Dios mío!" she said as she knelt beside her daughter. She pleaded with every breath for the intersession of all the saints she knew. When she saw the amount of blood her daughter was losing, she yelled out desperately to the storekeeper.

"Get me some *aceite*," she cried, unable to steady her voice as she called for kerosene.

The storekeeper raced to his store, called the sheriff and returned quickly with a can of kerosene. He unscrewed the cap and handed it to Viola.

"Por Dios," he said apprehensively looking on. "What are you going to do with that?" He watched in horror as she poured the kerosene onto to her daughter's chest.

"Get the sugar," Viola sobbed as she looked down at her hands covered in her daughter's blood. "Look on the kitchen table! *¡Apúrate!* Hurry!"

Someone handed her a large sugar bowl with no lid. Viola poured the sugar directly onto Rosa's chest and it quickly soaked up the bloody kerosene. She grabbed her apron and pressed down on her daughter's body with her elbows locked. She prayed that what worked for stanching the bleeding of castrated cattle and horses would work for her daughter now.

After what seemed like an eternity, someone outside the door shouted.

"Let me through! It is Dr. Esquibel!"

<hr />

Rosa survived the assault. She spent several weeks in bed, moving only to go to the bathroom or to sit at the table to eat some soup that her mother or grandmother brought her. Mostly she lay with her forearm across her eyes, as though the light was too strong for her. She said very little, except "Where's Miguel?" It took her weeks to heal but much longer to feel safe.

Ray went to see his sister after his appointment at the Ferguson Ranch. He found her sitting up in a chair near the window.

"How are you, Rosie?"

Rosa shrugged her shoulders and winced at the pain of moving muscles that had been damaged. She held her left arm against her body.

"I'll be okay. Have you seen him?"

"You mean Miguel? I heard he was in jail."

"I didn't think he could do it, Ray. I thought he was just a big talker. I shouldn't have called his bluff." She stared out the window across from her bed.

"It wouldn't have mattered, Rosa. That crazy son of a bitch wanted to hurt you. It was only a matter of time."

"How do you know, Ray?"

"I hear people talk."

"What do people say?"

"It's not important, Rosa. What does the doctor say about your recovery?" He wanted to change the subject.

"He says Mama's quick action saved me from bleeding to death. I'll be okay. But now I'm damaged goods. Men won't like to look at me anymore. They'll feel sorry for me when they see the scars," she said, her voice breaking.

"I think you should stop worrying about what men think."

Rosa stared out the window.

"Ray? Do you think you could get a note to Miguel for me?"

"Why? What are you trying to do?"

"I want to tell him that I'm sorry."

"Sorry for what, for trying to kill you?" Ray was getting impatient.

"It was my fault. If I hadn't been fooling around with Benny…" she paused.

"Okay. What do you want to say to him?

"I want to ask him to forgive me."

Ray shook his head.

"He tried to kill you, remember?"

"I don't think he really meant to hurt me so bad," she said. "He could have shot me. That little knife he cleaned his nails with wasn't really a weapon."

"I think you're lucky that bastard didn't stab you in the neck. I don't understand you, Rosa."

"Please, Ray."

"Okay, write your note and I'll see that he gets it. His cousin can probably take it to him."

Rosa wrote a note and put it into an envelope for Ray to take to Miguel. She told him she was sorry that she had been unfaithful to him. He deserved better. She said she wished she could have loved him like he loved her. She asked him for forgiveness and signed her name, Rosa Romero.

19.

THE MAN HAD BEEN GOING into Albuquerque every couple of months to visit 'his friend,' as he referred to her. She lived in the Anderson Heights area of Albuquerque with a panoramic view of the undeveloped land that stretched toward the western sunset. She was in her early twenties, about five-feet-two, with long dark hair. She had an apartment where she stayed during the day to rest before going out at night to work the eight pm to eight am shift at the 7-Eleven on Central near University.

That's how they met. He was buying some gas for his truck and she needed a ride. His charm put her at ease, especially his self-deprecating comments about his inexperience. He liked dancing with her to music from the radio. He started coming by early so he could be there when she got ready for work.

Tonight he seemed more anxious than usual. He sat on her bed to wait while she went to the bathroom. She left the door slightly ajar so he could see her preparations. She slipped out of her clothes then turned to the sink, bending forward slightly to wash her hands. He could see her breasts, the roundness of her body and her smooth legs. She was beautiful and knew that he was appreciating the view.

"Why haven't you asked me to make love?" she said as she walked toward him and sat next to him on the bed.

He stood up nervously then went to the window to look at the sunset.

"I guess I was waiting for the right time," he replied.

"I have a couple of hours before I need to be at work," she suggested. He looked at her and smiled.

"Two hours is a lifetime," he said and walked back to the bed where she was sitting.

She hadn't told him she was pregnant; that would have spoiled the mood. After all, the child wasn't his so she didn't see how that knowledge would change anything between them. He put his arm around her and firmly laid her back on the bed.

Her remains were the fifth uncovered at the mesa. With them was the four-month-old fetus of her unborn baby.

20.

RAY WAS SHOCKED and saddened when he heard that his grandfather, Don Patricio, had died. The old gentleman had been out in his garden hoeing the chile when he suffered a heart attack. No one knew he was ailing, but his love of cigarettes was a contributing factor in his death. A funeral was held at the Sangre de Christo Catholic Church and people came from miles around to pay their respects. Don Patricio's World War II buddies showed up all the way from Missouri. Felix Silva and his son Felix Jr. came from Bernalillo, as did many other legendary and colorful characters who had known Don Patricio in his day. Doña Virginia, Ray's grandmother, did not want to stay alone in the house and she didn't want to move in with José and Viola, so she went to live with her younger sister, Estella, in Denver. Ray and Rosa would have to travel a distance if they wanted to see her.

Ray and Rosa had been treated especially well by their grandparents, so it came as no surprise that when Doña Virginia moved to Denver, she left her house to her grandchildren. Don Patricio and she had discussed it many times because they wanted to make sure that the children had a place to live if anything ever happened to José or Viola. Rosa grieved the loss of her grandparents and appreciated their generosity, but she wasn't ready to leave the casita just yet.

The stabbing of her daughter and the sudden death of her father-in-law left Viola with a peculiar sense of dread. She couldn't seem to shake the feeling that something terrible was about to happen. She pleaded with Rosa to come back and stay with her at the house, but Rosa kept refusing.

"Mama, I've caused enough trouble for you. I need to stay in my own place," she said.

"You're no trouble, hija," said Viola. "I can cook for you and take care of your place until you're feeling stronger."

"No, mama, you have enough to do at home," insisted Rosa.

"You're not safe by yourself," said Viola.

"Miguel is in jail, mama. He can't hurt me now."

"Ay, hija. You worry me to death," said Viola. "You are so stubborn."

José seemed to settle down and drink less after his father died. He didn't change his activities much, but he was calmer and put more of his energy into running the tienda and maintaining the property. He was happy that his mother had left the house to Ray and Rosa because that assured him the property would stay in the family.

He also began to spend more time in Albuquerque and farther north. One of his favorite places to go was Silva's Saloon in Bernalillo. His father, Don Patricio, and Felix Silva Sr. had known each other for years and were great friends. In fact, Don Patricio went on a couple of bootlegging runs with Silva back in the days of prohibition. He loved telling stories about the trip from Bernalillo to Oklahoma City in Felix's old pickup with a cutout filled with straw and the whiskey. Don Patricio laughed when he talked about the trail of straw they left behind them on the first ten miles of highway. He said he was sure Felix was going to get caught one day, but he never did. José liked to visit old Felix's saloon not only for the atmosphere and liquor, but because he felt welcome there and could find a poker game going on in the back most weekends.

One Friday evening, José drove to Bernalillo to see if there was anything going on at Silva's. He hadn't seen Felix Silva since his father's funeral and when he arrived, Felix welcomed him with a drink on the house. They made small talk for a few minutes then José cocked his head towards the back room, and asked about a game. Felix motioned him to follow and opened a door that blended into the wall, disguised by the photos, old calendars, farm implements, racy drawings and photos of naked women, bills with signatures scribbled across them and license plates from various states that papered the entire interior of the saloon. He led him to the back room where a game of Texas Hold 'em was in full swing. The air above the table was a blue haze from the cigar and cigarette smoke and faces under the hats were barely visible. Felix walked over and said something to one of the players and then left. The player pulled up a chair and made room for José. They all eyed him briefly.

José was dealt two cards. He cautiously raised one corner to see what he was holding then folded. The others played their hands and in that time, José sized them up more for their identities than for their playing ability. He knew only two of the players. Pablo Montaño was an acquaintance from the horse-trading business. He'd come in from Peñasco. Leonél Marquez was big in the farming business and had driven in from Belén. The rest were most likely locals, except for one man. He wore a Chicago Cubs baseball cap and had a scruffy face. He was the only Anglo at the table. He wasn't smoking but was drinking something that smelled like Scotch. The dealer position had rotated to the player on his left. There were five cards on the table to pick from.

"Hey, Gabacho," said one of the locals. "You gonna bet or what?" The man sniffed and pushed in his chips.

The game was starting to get good. José now had a queen and a five and figured he could pick up two more fives and a king from the table for a decent hand. He checked. Someone folded, someone raised, the pot grew and the players went around again. By the turn there was a showdown between José and Pablo. José showed his hand, a queen of spades and five of hearts, so his best hand was three fives, a king and a queen. Pablo had a king and a jack making his final hand two pairs, kings and fives, with a jack kicker–not enough to win. José reached for the pot.

Another game would start soon but in the meantime, the men got up to stretch their legs, use the facilities and grab another drink from the bar. The man with the Cubs cap remained at the table sipping his Scotch.

"You're not from here," said José. "What's your name, hombre?"

"What's it to you?" was the reply.

"Hey, buddy. Just trying to make friendly conversation," said José, "before I take your money." José laughed.

The man looked up at José from under the bill of his cap. He had a cold, black stare. He didn't acknowledge the humor. Instead he grabbed his glass, got out of his chair and went out front to the bar. José took the opportunity to go to the men's room while everyone was stretching and getting their drinks refreshed. He walked past the bar area and the man in the cap tipped his glass in a sort of salute to Felix, and set it down on the counter.

The door to the men's room was two paces and a ninety degree angle to the pay phone. José went in and a minute later was preparing to exit when he heard part of a conversation. He pushed the door open a small crack and saw the man in the baseball cap with his back turned talking on the pay phone.

"Where's the bull?" said the man's voice. "You guys are having too much fun with this shit. Just do it and call me. You have the number."

José closed the door and went back to the sink to run some water. He washed his hands and stepped out of the men's room. He wondered what the telephone call was about, but he didn't much like the Anglo, so he kept it to himself. He decided to play one more hand before going home. The dealer was shuffling the deck and was about to deal, when the commotion in the bar started. The players got up and went out front to see what was going on.

Three men who had been hunting unsuccessfully up North were already drunk when they came into the saloon. Felix had a habit of leaning forward with his elbows on the bar to connect with his customers. The men were cursing and generally combative as they took their seats and when Felix leaned in to take their orders, one of the men slugged him in the eye. The other customers who witnessed the attack rushed to Felix's rescue, ready for a fight, but Felix wouldn't have it.

"You guys lock the front door and the rest of you block the back exit. Don't let these cabrones out of here," ordered Felix. "I'll take care of them." He grabbed a length of steel pipe from behind the counter and in one deft motion sprang out from behind the bar and started swinging. By the time it was over, there were three men lying on the floor with bloody heads and faces. Someone picked up the pay phone and called the sheriff.

When the excitement was over, José was ready for another game, so he looked around to see which players were left. He noticed that everyone except the Anglo man was still hanging around. In a few minutes the police siren could be heard, so several players went to the back and cleaned up the poker table. They pushed the table against the wall and put some chairs on its surface with the legs up. They returned to the main room and scattered about the bar with their drinks in hand. As much as he would have liked to stay longer, José finished his drink and returned to Los Lunas after midnight.

21.

CATE FERGUSON CALLED RAY on a Saturday morning with a problem. He offered to drive to her ranch if she didn't mind waiting until two o'clock. She agreed. Ray already had a meeting scheduled with her for the following week but she sounded disturbed and he was curious. When he arrived at the Ferguson Ranch, he drove up to the main house and she met him on the portal.

"What's going on?" he asked.

She was clearly nervous and sat on a bench, but she kept looking up at him not knowing how to start.

"Is something wrong, Cate?"

"I think so, I mean, yes," she said.

Ray strolled over and sat next to her.

"Are you going to tell me?" he said gently.

"It's my brother. He's back from Chicago."

"I wasn't aware you have a brother," said Ray.

"He's my half-brother, actually, one of my father's early indiscretions."

"I see. What's his name?"

"Jack. He's about ten years older than I am."

"What does Jack do?"

"Honestly, I don't know."

"So what's the problem?"

"Jack came in late last night, saying he's going to take over the herd."

"You mean the Charolais?"

"Those are my cattle, Ray. Dad wanted me to breed them. It's why I went to vet school."

Her voice rose, displaying her level of exasperation.

"Take it easy," said Ray. "Do you know what he plans to do with them?"

"He said I was turning them into pets and that he planned to make a change."

"What do you think he means by that?"

"He said something about letting them go feral to toughen them up."

"He has to take them away from here to do it, doesn't he?"

"That's just it. I think he wants to lay claim to the property in Clovis."

Ray was silent. He had barely started the property assessment for the probate hearing and he could see a problem looming if the heirs began to make property grabs.

"I'm not an attorney, Cate, but I think you should get one you trust to file an injunction on your behalf and stop your brother from taking the cattle–for starters, anyway."

"I can call my godfather. He's a lawyer and he's never trusted Jack. Thank you for coming out here, Ray. I was so upset I just didn't know who to talk to."

There was a racket out in the lane and a black Jeep Wrangler pulled up. The man inside wore a Cubs baseball cap and stepped out of the vehicle with an air of someone accustomed to being in control. He strode onto the portal.

"Who's this, Cate? One of your vet friends?" he asked sarcastically.

"No, as a matter of fact, but he is a friend."

"Why don't you tell your friend to move along? You and I have to talk."

"Whatever you have to say to me you can say with him here," said Cate, looking at Ray.

"I see. When's the wedding?" said her brother.

"Ray's the accountant that was hired to do the property assessment. If you have plans involving this estate, you'd better put them on the table right now," she replied in a steady voice.

The two men eyed each other.

"What the fuck, Cate. I already told you what I'm going to do. You can't stop me, so why are we playing games?"

"Show a little respect for the lady," said Ray. "She has a say in what happens around here."

Jack repressed the urge to get up in Ray's face, but stood his ground without saying another word. He bit the inside of his lower lip and barged into the house.

"I guess you'd better go, Ray," said Cate. "I'll be all right. Thanks for coming. I'll call you on Tuesday."

Ray was reluctant to leave Cate under her present circumstances, but he knew he wasn't going to help matters between her and her brother. He drove away wondering why fate had thrust him into the lives of women he had to worry about.

22.

RAY WAS WORKING HARD at his job in Public Accounting, performing financial audits and offering advisory services to clients. He had recently been hired by a small Albuquerque auto-parts store to help them assess the company's performance after three years of being in business. They kept poor records, and his first task was to reconcile their accounting information and prepare a financial report. He had been totally focused on building a balance sheet when he got a call from his mother. As soon as he heard her voice, he knew something had happened. She told him his father had died.

Ray took a few days off to go to Los Lunas. When he arrived in town, he found his childhood friend, Pete Estrada, waiting for him.

"Ray, buddy, I'm sorry about your old man, no?" said Pete sadly looking down at his own feet.

"How did it happen, Pete?" Ray asked.

"I guess your dad was helping some friends who were breeding one of their mares to a stallion from Corrales, no." Pete had the habit of saying 'you know?' which he shortened to 'no?' as he talked.

"What friends?"

"That McAdams guy, you know him. They call him Mac, no? He owns the dairy here in town. I guess he's into horses, too."

"What's so special about the stallion?" asked Ray.

"I don't know but somebody said that Comanchero, that's the horse's name, had made a name for himself racing in the small towns along the Rio Grande, no? He's a big guy—about seventeen hands. Anyway, I heard that his breeding rights. . ."

"So what happened, Pete?" Ray interrupted.

"Of course, sorry, sorry," Pete said. "On the day of the breeding the mare was already confined down at the dairy when Johnny Trujillo brought his horse trailer in from Corrales, no? You could tell that horse was mean just by the trouble they had unloading him from the trailer. He was jumpy, rolling his eyes, and kept rearing, no? He was a sight to see!"

Ray listened intently without expression as Pete told the story.

"That poor mare," said Pete as he shook his head. "She paced back and forth raising her head to sniff the air and rolling her eyes at Comanchero, no? Mac asked your dad to help, I guess, because your dad is good with horses. Your dad had the mare by the rope but she wasn't holding steady. Johnny brought his horse in on a long tether, so your dad let out the mare's line, and backed away as far as he could. That was when all hell broke loose, no? The stallion reared up and came down kicking and hit the side of the pen. He went in a circle kicking out just like a bucking bronco, no? Your dad pulled in the slack trying to turn the mare, but she reared up. That poor horse was terrified. The horses did this dance for a few minutes then they sort of calmed down. I swear to God, Ray!" said Pete pausing to swallow and take a breath. "No one saw it coming, no?"

Pete shook his head, looking as though he was going to cry. He looked directly at Ray to reinforce his sincerity, and swallowed hard. His voice quavered as he began talking again. Ray continued to stare at him without saying a word.

"Damn that Comanchero!" Pete said. "He turned so quickly that Johnny couldn't hold him. The horse put his head down and slashed out with his back legs, no? Your dad caught both hooves right in the chest."

Pete brought his palms up and emphatically slammed them against his chest.

"Your dad went backwards and hit the dirt–¡SAS!" exclaimed Pete, describing the sound made by José's body as it hit the ground. He paused for a respectful moment of silence and to regain his composure.

"The mare was loose and she took off, no?" he continued. "Johnny grabbed his horse and pulled him back to the trailer. We all rushed over to your dad, but he didn't move."

Pete shook his head slowly from side to side.

"We called the ambulance right away, but it was too late. I'm sorry, Bro."

Ray was moved by the story of his father's death, but he had no real reaction to the fact he was gone. Pete reached over and patted him on the shoulder.

"You okay, buddy?" Pete asked him.

"Yes," Ray replied stiffening a bit. "What a hell of a thing," he said without emotion.

"Is the funeral next week?" asked Pete.

"You'll see it in the paper," said Ray.

He stood in silence for a minute, nodded awkwardly to Pete, then walked away toward his car.

The funeral of José Martinez was the event of the year in Los Lunas. Although he had no close friends, he had many acquaintances who came to pay their respects from as far north as Bernalillo and as far south as El Paso. In addition to the many family members, there were horsemen, farmers, gambling buddies, businessmen and others that no one really recognized. Surprisingly, there were several women there who did not get in the line to pay their respects, but walked up to the coffin single file and wept quietly as they stood beside his body. Family members looked at one another, shaking their heads and speculating in whispery voices about the women. Luis stood at the back of the church with his arms crossed and surveyed the mourners. One young woman in her twenties came in with a small child, a boy about six years old. The boy dressed like a cowboy looked like a miniature version of José. The whispers grew a bit louder and someone questioned if Viola had known about the child.

In the front pew of the small church sat Ray, Rosa and Viola. Ray wore a conservative dark suit for the occasion. Viola was dressed in black with a mantilla over her head. She barely moved and her grief was difficult to define. The solemn event was punctuated by sniffling, nose blowing and occasional whimpers from the congregation but she sat without expression. Rosa sat next to her mother and, in contrast, blazed like a candle in a red dress with a lace overlay and shoes to match. Her choice of color for her father's funeral raised the eyebrows of people who assumed it was because of her flashy ways. Most of the women were critical.

Toward the end of the mass, Father Reyes spoke eloquently about José, emphasizing the themes of redemption and forgiveness.

"Our brother José Martinez was not a perfect man. No one in this place is perfect, including myself," said the priest. "But God is almighty and forgives us for our weaknesses, and so should we also forgive others. If anyone here holds anger or blame toward José, let us release him by forgiving him in our hearts at this time." The priest paused.

"And likewise," he began again. "We should ask our brother José to forgive us, if we ever hurt him in any way. Let us take a moment to ask José for that forgiveness."

The church grew quiet.

Rosa stared at the coffin during the silence. She had a blank expression on her face and had not shed any tears. She slowly got out of the pew, walked deliberately past the priest and stood next to her father's coffin. The crowd murmured and rustled nervously at such a daring breach of protocol. She hadn't spoken to her father in years but now she stood with her hands clenched and whispered something close to his face. She ran her hand down the front of her dress and tore off a piece of red lace and placed it across her father's mouth. Instead of returning to the pew, she walked out of the church.

Viola sat motionless next to Ray. Her fingers moved swiftly through her rosary as though nothing at all had happened. Ray shot a quick glance at her and saw that she had her eyes closed and was intently reciting the rosary prayers. It was unlikely she had noticed Rosa leave.

The priest was aghast. People looked at each other, grumbled and shook their heads disapprovingly as they turned to watch Rosa go. Father Reyes knew he had to wrap up the funeral quickly. He went to the coffin to give a last blessing to the deceased, and hesitated a moment when he saw the red lace. He discreetly pulled it away and tucked it under José's shoulder, then turned and faced the crowd. He directed a blessing to everyone, made a sign of the cross, then stepped aside so the funeral home staff could prepare the coffin for the procession.

23.

THE MAN DROVE onto an open expanse of dirt that stretched as far as the eye could see. A contractor long ago began clearing the land for development but the land remained undisturbed after all these years. He drove into the area from the north side where there was a gradual decline from the dunes to the expansive flat area below. The sky was black at that hour; a waning crescent moon cast a faint light. The man got out of the truck and unloaded some bags of trash, landscaping materials, shrubbery trimmings and some broken terra cotta pot shards. He climbed back into the truck and drove about a hundred yards farther west and parked the truck. He went around back and climbed into the bed of the truck to pull out a shovel. He threw the shovel over the side and jumped out after it. He started digging. The air smelled of rain coming and ozone from a not too distant lightning strike. He worked quickly in the soft, sandy dirt and dug a hole four feet by two feet by three feet deep.

After an hour of digging, he stopped and lowered the truck's tailgate. He removed a green tarp, wadded it up and tossed it to one side. Under the tarp was a cocoon-like form covered in black plastic and fastened around with tie-downs. He reached in for the black plastic and pulled it toward him until half of it was hanging down the tailgate.

He jumped down from the truck and grabbed the package at the middle and hiked it off the truck bed and over his shoulder. He carried the package and dropped it beside the hole. Quickly he released the tie downs and looped them through his belt. Opening the top flap so it dropped down the wall of the hole, he grabbed the opposite flap and lifted the plastic until the contents rolled into the hole. The naked body of a woman settled awkwardly in her grave.

Gathering the plastic, he roughly bunched it up and threw it into the truck. He pulled the tie-downs out of his belt and tossed them back there, as well. He shoveled the dirt back into the grave until it was completely filled, stepped on it until it was well compressed, then brushed the top with a few strokes of some nearby branches. He tossed the shovel back into the truck.

The faint glow of a distant skyline was visible beneath a bank of heavy clouds. He felt a drop of rain strike his forehead. Gathering the tarp and plastic into a rough wad, he fastened them with the tie-downs so they wouldn't blow out of the truck. He drove away and pulled out to the empty highway just in time for the rain to start coming down hard. He turned on the headlights and wipers and headed north.

24.

ROSA MOVED IN with her mother a few weeks after her father died. She arrived carrying a suitcase and a grocery sack filled with items from her own refrigerator. She put them down next to the kitchen door. She could see that her mother was out back sitting in a lawn chair on the porch overlooking the garden. Rosa hadn't been inside the house for almost two years. The place had fallen into disrepair and had a funky odor of dust and grime and an underlying scent of damp calcimine and old rose petal sachet. The geraniums had dried up and the vine in the kitchen window was losing its leaves. The kitchen was not clean, but did not appear to be used on a daily basis.

In the bedroom where her parents had slept, the bed was turned so that the orientation of the vigas was now lengthwise rather than crosswise the way she remembered it. She couldn't think of a good reason for that except it gave the sleeper a view out the window. The bed was covered with several thin quilts that her mother had made from remnants of what Rosa recognized as her father's old dress trousers and jackets. All of her mother's saints were clustered on the chest of drawers against the wall to the right of the bed. Rosa approached the collection and found seven small cards, each the size of a third of an index card, laid out side by side before the statues. Each card was marked only with a small black cross and a blue or pink flower—four of the flowers were blue. The name LUZ was written on the seventh card. Rosa picked up the card for a closer look and discovered that another card was beneath it. The card had no cross, only the name Rosita and a small pink heart drawn on it.

A lump formed in Rosa's throat as she realized that Rosita had been her own baby. Tears fell from her eyes as she was overcome with anguish for the first time. She put the cards back the way she found them and returned to the kitchen. She met her mother coming through the back door carrying some mint sprigs.

"I brought you some yerba buena to make tea, hija. I would like a cup myself," she said as she handed the sprigs to Rosa.

"Thank you, mama," said Rosa, gently, and put her arm around her mother's shoulder. "Let's see what we can fix for supper, too. Why don't you sit down while I see what there is."

The refrigerator was practically empty but Rosa had some cheese, dry pasta and canned milk in her grocery sack. She put a pot of water to boil on the stove for the pasta and threw a generous pinch of salt into the pot. Then she filled the kettle with tap water and started it to boil for the tea. Her mother sat in silence at the table, smoothing the wrinkles of the worn oil cloth table cover.

"Mama," said Rosa. "After dinner I can help you water your plants and pull weeds, if you want. Does that sound good?"

Her mother nodded slowly.

"What are you cooking, hija?" she asked.

"Macaroni and cheese Mama. I'll have to go to the store in the morning," said Rosa.

"Let me give you some money," said her mother. She got up from the chair, went into the bedroom and returned with a two-pound humidor of tobacco. She pried off the lid to reveal tightly rolled bills held by rubber bands stuffed inside the can. Rosa recognized the smell of her grandfather's burley tobacco as it wafted up to her nose.

"Mama!" she said. "Where did you get that?"

"Your grandpa gave it to me. He said I would need it someday."

"Where did it all come from?" asked Rosa, surprised at what appeared to be a fortune.

"You know, mija, your grandpa liked to play cards," she said as she unrolled one bundle of ten dollar bills. She handed it to Rosa.

"Here, hija. You go to the store and buy whatever you want."

Rosa accepted the money and watched her mother replace the lid on the humidor. She suddenly realized that her family was a complete mystery to her.

Rosa took on the care of her mother. She cooked, cleaned and handled things the way her mother had taught her. The house began to take on a lived-in look; the plants bounced back, even the red geraniums that Rosa thought were dead. She was pleased with her work.

Rosa decided she would have to learn how to drive her father's truck if she were to take proper care of her mother. She borrowed a copy of the Driver's Handbook and read it front to back each night after her mother was asleep. After a week of studying, she grabbed the keys to the truck and attempted to start it. It had not been driven in so long that it wouldn't start. She sat in the seat and looked at all the gauges, moved the seat so she could reach the pedals comfortably, adjusted the mirrors and worked the levers. She repeated each procedure until she understood the truck. All she needed now was a mechanic.

She walked the eighth of a mile down the road to Pete Estrada's house and went to the back where he had a shop and parked his green '59 Cadillac. Luckily, Pete was there changing the oil on his truck when she walked up.

"Hey, Rosa, what's happening, Chica?" he said wiping his oily hands on a red shop towel. "How's your mama doing?"

Pete was one of those people who, despite the crazy things he had done growing up, stayed loyal to his friends. Ray was his best friend of all time so by extension, Rosa had his friendship as well.

"Mama's doing okay, Pete. I came to ask you a favor," she said.

"Anything," said Pete. "You name it."

"Well, I can't seem to start my Papá's truck. Can you take a look at it?"

"No problem," he said. "Let me wash this stuff off my hands and get the keys to the Caddy."

In a few minutes Pete appeared with the keys to his car and offered Rosa a lift back to her house so he could see what was going on with the truck.

"I don't think I've ever ridden in a car like this," said Rosa admiring the dashboard. It had a clean, streamlined look with pairs of gauges to either side of the large but thin steering wheel. "What do you call this color?"

Pete sat up straighter in the driver's seat, pleased that a girl had shown interest in his car.

"They call this Acadian Green," he said proudly. "I restored it myself."

"You did a great job, Pete. They sure aren't making cars like these anymore," said Rosa.

By the time they reached Rosa's house, Pete was beaming.

"Let's have a look at this *troquita*," he said, referring to it as a little truck.

Pete climbed inside and found the keys still in the ignition. He pushed in the clutch and turned the key but got no response.

"I know what's wrong here," he said confidently. "The battery is dead, no? And I mean toes-up dead. When was the last time it was driven?"

"I think Ray drove it after Papá's funeral but it's been parked under this tree since then," said Rosa.

Pete shook his head and pondered for a moment, looping his thumbs through the chest straps of his overalls and rocking back and forth on his heels.

"I'll have to get a new battery, no? Lucky for you, I have one that I salvaged out of a truck I took to the auto bone yard," he said tapping his forehead to indicate that he was always thinking ahead. "I'll be right back."

While Pete was gone, Rosa went inside to check on her mother. She found her asleep in the lounge chair on the back porch. She put a shawl over her but otherwise left her undisturbed. She paused by the refrigerator, withdrew a pitcher of mint tea and poured two glasses for her and Pete. When he returned with the battery, she was standing by the truck with the glasses sitting on the tailgate.

"Is that a mint julep I'm seeing there?" he asked smacking his lips.

"Mint without the julep," said Rosa, laughing at his antics. "But it's cold and wet."

"Hey, Rosa, this is good stuff," he said taking several gulps and wiping his mouth on the cuff of his shirt. "Let's get to work."

In a few minutes, Pete had the old battery out and the new one installed. He climbed into the truck again, turned the key and started up the motor after a couple of attempts. He pressed the accelerator to hear what the engine sounded like, left it in neutral while he checked the lights and gauges, then he told Rosa to get in. As soon as she was in, he backed up the truck and drove it around the yard a couple of times and let Rosa out.

"Needs oil," he said, "and needs some fresh gas. You planning to drive this thing?"

Rosa nodded.

"I've been studying the manual. I need to learn how," she said.

"Okay, I got it," he exclaimed. "I'll drive the truck down to the station and put some gas and oil in it then I'll bring it back and show you how to drive it."

Rosa smiled gratefully and clasped her hands together like a child.

"You don't know what this means to me, Pete," she said.

"You can repay me with some more of that mint tea— with the julep next time," he said, grinning at her and driving off.

For the next two weeks Pete worked with Rosa until she could confidently drive the truck down Main Street. She mastered the clutch and shift quickly and only needed to learn how to parallel park. He drove her to take the test and she emerged from the building waving her new drivers' license in the air.

"How about a ride back home?" he said.

"I think I can manage that. Move over," she said smugly, and off they went.

25.

ONE MORNING A POLICE SERGEANT from Albuquerque knocked at the kitchen door and Rosa talked with him through the screen.

"Ma'm, are you Mrs. Romero? Mrs. Miguel Romero?" he asked, taking off his cap and placing it beneath his arm, military style.

Rosa had not been called by her married name for such a long time that she didn't think of herself as a married woman.

"Yes, I'm Miguel's wife," she said, apprehensively. "Has something happened to him?"

"No, ma'm," said the police officer. "He's being released next week and we want to know if you are going to be safe."

"It's very kind of you to come, Sergeant," said Rosa noticing the unpronounceable name that started with a Z on his name tag. "I don't believe he is a dangerous person."

"He tried to kill you, ma'm," said the officer. "Aren't you worried he will try again? You could file a restraining order against him."

"I don't think so," said Rosa. "I would like to see him, though. Is that possible?"

The sergeant stared at her and raised his eyebrows.

"Well, yes, ma'm. You can. It will have to be Monday or Tuesday because he's getting out on Wednesday," he said.

"All right," said Rosa. "Thank you, Sergeant."

The officer nodded.

"Good day to you, ma'm," he said, donning his cap and walking away from the house.

Rosa had not seen Miguel in almost a year. The visit from the police sergeant had stirred up the memory of that terrible day and she wondered how Miguel felt toward her now, after all this time. She also thought of poor Benny. He disappeared altogether and someone else was making his deliveries to Los Lunas. She'd heard that he went back to Texas. Rosa sighed. A tight feeling crept into her throat, but she resolved to go to the detention center to see Miguel before he got out.

On Monday Rosa drove herself to Albuquerque. She was more apprehensive about driving in the city than seeing Miguel. She found her way to the detention center and managed to park the truck in the visitor parking lot. She approached the desk inside the building and stated her business, proud that she could present her new license as identification.

She waited a few minutes, until someone appeared to escort her through the locked doors into the room where the inmates met with visitors.

Rosa sat nervously as she waited for Miguel to appear. When he did, she saw that his black hair was cut close to his head and he wore an orange jumpsuit with white socks and rubber sandals. He had aged during his time in lockup, and his good looks had hardened into wariness. He seemed happy to see her.

"Rosa," he said. "I guess you heard that I'm getting out this week."

"I heard," she replied. "How are you doing, Miguel?"

Miguel looked down and stifled a disdainful snort.

"I've been better." He looked up at her and stared at the scar on her bare arm.

"Did you get my letter?" asked Rosa.

He nodded his head.

"Miguel, I don't have anything to fear from you, do I?"

He stared at her again. His eyes softened a bit.

"You're still my wife," he said.

"That's why I'm here, Miguel. I'm not the same person anymore."

"You want a divorce?" he asked.

Rosa nodded.

"I think it's the best thing to do. We just remind each other of the past. You'll probably want to move away from here," said Rosa.

"I see you're still trying to tell me what to do!" he snapped.

"See what I mean, Miguel? It just won't work between us."

Miguel shook his head and worked his palm against the edge of the metal table.

"Okay, but tell me one thing?" he asked.

"What is it?" Rosa replied.

"Did you love me even a little bit?"

Rosa sighed and looked at him.

"We had lots of fun, Miguel. Truthfully, I don't really know what love is."

He pursed his lips as he thought about what she had said.

"I heard your dad died," he said, not looking up, but continuing to rub the table, this time with his forefinger. "They said you wore a red dress to the funeral."

Rosa showed no reaction.

"I'd sure like to see you in that red dress," said Miguel, smiling.

"Don't have it anymore," said Rosa. "Even if I did, why would I wear it for you?"

Miguel stared at her but had nothing more to say.

"I'll have the divorce papers ready tomorrow. I think it's best if you don't come around," Rosa said with finality.

The guard stepped up and Miguel rose to go.

"Miguel?" said Rosa. "I forgive you."

He looked askance at her for a few seconds then left the room ahead of the guard.

Rosa's mother was haunted as ever and did not seem to thrive. She sat at the kitchen table and stared into the yard hardly talking with Rosa. Occasionally, she would go out back to water her herb garden and reposition the two lawn chairs that sat on the porch. She continually looked worried, as though her vigilance would soon reveal whatever she feared most. She spent time at night in front of her saints, praying novenas until she was too tired to stand.

Rosa knew her mother was depressed and felt she was disappearing faster than anyone could keep track. Viola was unable to communicate except at the most basic level, and eventually Rosa became detached, convincing herself that feeding and bathing her mother were the only important requirements. Her mother felt the disinterest keenly and that triggered bouts of hysteria, followed by catatonic episodes as her mind slowly eroded by dementia. Rosa began to spoon feed her. She kept asking for tea but never drank what Rosa provided. Instead her mother stirred the cup incessantly until Rosa had to take it away just to break the aggravating sound of the spoon circling against ceramic.

Viola spent the last days of her life in her room surrounded by her saints and mementos, lying on the bed where she had endured so much abuse from José. The priest came to give her the Last Rites but she never spoke again. She died with her eyes open, staring at the dark vigas on the ceiling above her bed.

Rosa keenly felt the loss of her mother. They had been through so much together and Rosa felt that she really understood her mother. She had no doubt that her mother loved her and Ray but she was sad about the fact that she had never achieved whatever dreams she might have had in life. She arranged a modest funeral for her and was surprised that many people she had never met attended. Many of them were from the church but there was a group from a gardening club and another from a local organization that helped the poor. It made her think about her own aspirations. She was alone again, but soon she would have to think about what she wanted to do with her own life.

26.

RAY LOST HIS PARENTS and grandfather in such a short period of time that he questioned his ability to concentrate on his work. He met with his supervisor and asked him if he could turn the Ferguson portfolio over to a colleague. His supervisor agreed but Ray felt that he should inform Cate Ferguson personally. Besides, he had the urge to see her one more time. He left for the ranch the next day, and arrived there about noon.

Ray noticed as he arrived that the cattle were not in the field, as they had been the previous times he'd been there. The gate was open and someone was plowing the sod under with a tractor. He parked at the ranch house and walked across the lane to the open gate and stared at the activity. Ray figured the land was being prepared to plant hay for the cattle. A gentle hand on his shoulder startled him as he turned to see Cate standing behind him.

"They're all gone, Ray, every single one."

"What happened?"

"I couldn't fight him. He said he was dad's oldest and deserved to have what was rightfully his."

"But I thought you were going to talk to your lawyer friend."

"I did, but Jack convinced him that I wasn't cut out for raising cattle. Do you know that I graduated at the top of my class with research in animal reproduction and biotechnology, and he had the nerve to tell me that I would be better off working for one of the boutique veterinary practices in town?"

"I'm sorry, Cate. I wish I could have done more."

"Don't be sorry. If it hadn't been for this mess, I never would have met you."

She smiled at him, her eyes brightening. Ray felt a bit shy.

"How would you like to grab a bite to eat? I know this great little place not too far from here where they make—

"Cate," Ray interrupted. "I came to tell you that I'm handing your portfolio off to someone else."

She stared at him and disappointment clouded her gaze.

"Why? You've been doing such a great job."

"It's not you, if that's what you're thinking. I didn't tell you, but I lost my parents and my grandfather in the span of a few months and I need some time off."

"I'm so sorry, Ray. I guess my problems seem pale by comparison."

"Not at all. I wanted you to keep your cattle. I hate to say it but I didn't like your brother. He reminds me of those Chicago gangsters you see in movies."

"You wouldn't be the first person to say that. It's just that he's not really from here."

"Could that Cubs cap be a clue?" said Ray, laughing softly.

"He said he won it playing poker and he never goes anywhere without it. Who knows what the truth really is."

"I'll tell you what. When things settle down for me, I'd like to see you again. We can go eat at your special little restaurant…deal?"

"Don't take too long. A lot can happen around here before you know it." She smiled and put out her hand to him.

Ray impulsively brought her hand to his lips in a courtly manner and made eye contact with her. She smiled.

"I hope we're going to be great friends, Ray."

"I think we already are," replied Ray. "See you later."

Ray felt like visiting his Uncle Luis who lived on Osuna Avenue, not too far out of Ray's way returning from the Ferguson Ranch. He felt a need to make contact with the living members of his family. Ray found him in his backyard unloading bags of manure, potting soil and mulch from his pickup. His uncle was surprised to see him.

"Ramón!" he called out loudly. "To what do I owe the pleasure?"

"Hi, Uncle," said Ray.

"Cómo que, hi, Uncle? Get over here, muchacho and greet your Tío properly," said Luis as he gave him a high five then grabbed Ray around the shoulder.

Ray smiled and allowed his uncle to hug him, but he quickly returned to a more formal interaction with him.

"I'm working in Albuquerque now," said Ray. "I thought I should come and visit."

"Welcome, welcome, muchacho. The last time I saw you, you were no bigger than a jackrabbit."

Ray smirked.

"I think I was a little bigger than that, Unc. . . Tío," he corrected himself.

"Tell me about your job. You already graduated from college and everything?"

"Yes. I'm a CPA now—working downtown," said Ray.

"I used to tell your mama, that boy is going to be somebody in this world. Smart kid, smart," said Luis tapping his finger on Ray's head.

"Mama told me about that, Tío."

"I'm sure sorry about your mama," said Luis. "She was a good woman. José didn't deserve her." He shook his head.

Ray didn't respond, keeping his opinion to himself.

"How about it, muchacho? You got a nice girl yet?" Luis asked, turning to pick up a roll of landscaping plastic. He grunted as he heaved the heavy roll onto the bed of the truck.

"Not yet, Tío. I've got a few friends, though."

"Friends?" Luis stopped in mid-stoop and turned to look at him. "You aren't hanging around those bad girls, are you, hijo? Those girls are no good for nothing." He continued unloading sacks.

"No, Tío. I remember what you said about girls being impossible to satisfy. I've met a few like that."

"Don't go messing with them," admonished his uncle. "You could catch something."

Ray felt a mild wave of disgust pass through him but said nothing.

"How about something to drink, muchacho?" asked his uncle.

"I'll take a Coke if you have one," said Ray.

"Sure. Come inside," said his uncle.

Ray followed his uncle inside. The house was meticulous, with everything in place. Luis walked to the kitchen, grabbed two cold Cokes from the refrigerator and handed one to Ray. He snapped up the tab and slugged down several gulps. Ray did the same but drank more slowly.

"Nice place you keep here, Tío," said Ray.

'Thank you, thank you, I can't stand a filthy house," said Luis, shrugging his shoulders and shaking his head to show disgust.

Ray walked toward a corner cabinet with glass shelves and looked at a few trophies displayed there.

"Did you play ball?" he asked.

"You mean the trophies? I've had those since I was a kid. Used to be pretty good at baseball," said Luis.

Ray thought that his uncle must be living in the past, with all those trophies on display.

"Mama said you were married," said Ray.

"I was, twice, but like I tell you, you just can't satisfy women. They spent all my money and gave me nothing but grief. I'm better off alone."

"Hmm."

"Make yourself at home, buddy," said Luis. "I've got to use the facilities."

While Luis was gone Ray continued to look at the knickknacks on the shelves. A four-inch square box like those he'd seen brought up from Juarez, made from pieces of stained glass leaded together, had its lid slightly ajar. Ray looked back to see if his uncle was coming and opened the lid. Inside was a tangle of women's jewelry, mostly earrings and chains, but prominently sitting on top, and the reason that the lid wouldn't close, was a silver cross with a little window in the center. Ray had seen that cross before, but he didn't remember where. He heard the toilet flush so he put the lid down and turned his attention to a velvet painting of a matador and bull on the opposite wall.

"What do you think, muchacho? You ever wished you could be one of those guys?" said Luis, pointing with his chin at the picture.

"Not at all, Tío. Seems like a risky way to make a living."

"But that's the excitement of it! Getting up close and personal with a dangerous creature like that. Taking its life–that has to be a thrill!" Luis's passion flared, and tapered off quickly.

"How's work, Tío?" asked Ray, changing the subject. "Have you got plenty of business here?"

"Ray, I got more business than I know what to do with. In fact, just the other day I got into it with my boss because he said the fees for dumping were cutting into his profits.

He wanted me to double up on the loads. I told him if I got fined for overloading it would cost him more than the extra trips. He's an asshole. I didn't push it. I figured out how to cut corners to make ends meet. What do you say, Ray? Want to stay for lunch?"

"No, thanks," said Ray. "I've got to get going. I'm going to Los Lunas to see Rosa."

"Rosa de Castilla, what a beautiful girl. You tell her Uncle Luis sends his regards."

Ray headed for the door. Luis was right behind him and paused to grab a shovel that had fallen against the jamb. He threw it into the truck.

"Come back and see me anytime Ramón," he said.

Ray put out his hand for a high five. Luis nodded in approval and reciprocated.

"See you, Tío."

Ray thought about his uncle all the way back to Los Lunas. Ever since he had seen him at the State Fair that one time, he couldn't seem to reconcile what seemed like a contradiction between his uncle's words about women and the actions Ray had observed. Thinking about it made him sigh, especially now since he had visited him at home. Ray concluded that his uncle was a complicated person and that he probably would never really understand him, especially since he had no desire to visit him more frequently.

27.

"RAY!" SHOUTED ROSA and erupted in a giggle as she pulled open the kitchen door. "Come in!"

She grabbed a chair for him.

"Sit over here," she said. "I'll get you something to drink."

"No, no, Rosie," he said. "Don't trouble yourself. I can't stay too long. I just came to see how you're getting along."

"Lindo," she said and smiled. "Look around. The place is looking pretty good, don't you think?"

"It really does," said Ray. He noticed how clean and tidy everything was. He especially noticed that gardenia-like smell of the vine blooming in the window that took him right back to his early childhood.

"What have you been doing with yourself?" asked Rosa.

He responded with a broad, generous grin.

"Have a new client," he said, as he held her gaze. He wanted to tell her about Catherine Ferguson, but there was nothing much to say except that he was sort of attracted to her.

"Ah, you know," he said dismissively, "the usual stuff. I've been cleaning up other people's finances. I did about forty tax returns last week."

"Forty! Isn't that about all the people in town?" she laughed with an overtone of sarcasm.

"Just about," he smirked. "People don't know much about where their money goes. Throw in a trip to Las Vegas and, well, you can guess the rest."

"This was why you're the best in town," she remarked. "You tell them how to count their horses and cattle for tax purposes and what their odds will be at the racetrack. You help them figure the acreage of their alfalfa fields, their crops and their orchards, and the amount of produce and eggs they have to take to the farmers' market to make a profit. What more could a self-respecting farmer ask for?"

"You're right, Rosa. I guess that's all I'm cut out to do," he said, with a crooked grin.

She rose from her chair and started toward the refrigerator.

"Where are you going?" he asked her.

"To get you some tea," she said. "What sort of a host do you think I am?"

"I had a Coke earlier. Just sit down and talk to me," he said with his characteristic impatience.

"Well, I learned how to drive," she said, sitting back down and looking up at him.

"How did that happen?" he asked, surprised.

"Pete helped me," she said. "You know, Ray, he really is a great friend. He thinks you hang the moon."

"I know," said Ray. "He sort of got left behind when I went away to school."

"He put a new battery, some oil and some gas in the truck. And, he took me to get my license."

"Rosa, you aren't thinking about getting hooked up with Pete, are you?"

"Pete? No," she said emphatically. "I don't think he's interested in me that way."

"All men are interested in you that way, Rosa," said her brother in his best assessor's tone.

"No, not anymore," she said regretfully. "But I am a single woman again." She brightened.

"Miguel gave me a divorce." She let the weight of her statement settle for a minute.

"Did he give you a hard time about it?" asked Ray.

"No. I went to see him a couple of days before he got out."

"Where is he now?" asked Ray feeling a bit of concern for Rosa's safety.

"I honestly don't know, but I'm not afraid of him. Besides he's not going to do anything stupid while he's on parole."

"I hope not," said Ray. "What else is on your mind, Rosie?"

Rosa faced her brother, but looked down at her hands in silence.

"I've been thinking about Mama," she said.

"What's there to think about? She's gone and nothing can change that."

She looked at him, her expression serious and distant.

"I know, I know," she said, pausing. "I've been trying to remember how she made soup."

"Soup? Are you hungry?"

"No, Ray, but I keep remembering things she did so I don't forget her."

"How will you forget her living here?" suggested Ray.

"It's not that. I just really miss her, I guess." Her voice trailed off as she remembered something else. "She was really sick that last year. She just stared into space like she had already gone somewhere else. As hard as Papá had been on her, I wonder if she still loved him."

"She really did go someplace else, Rosa. She lost her mind. You couldn't have done anything more than you did. What's still bothering you?"

"I don't know," she replied, wringing her hands. "I just keep seeing her face."

"Are you worried that you'll end up like her?" Ray asked.

"I don't know, Ray. I don't want to. I just don't know."

"You're still grieving, Rosa. It will take time."

"I never got to thank her, Ray. She did so much for me. I never told her all of it."

Her eyes became teary.

"All of what?" asked Ray with increased concern.

"I never told her about Papá. How he hurt me."

"How did he hurt you?" asked Ray, feeling perturbed.

"I didn't want to hurt her. I wonder now if somehow she might have known," Rosa continued.

"Known what, Rosa? You're talking in riddles," said Ray, now exasperated.

"Papá got me pregnant, Ray," she said looking up at him and directly into his eyes.

"What are you talking about, Rosa?"

"It was the night I sneaked out to go to the Fair with Miguel. Papá was drunk and caught me sneaking back into the house. He beat me, Ray. He hurt my head." She paused, and said, "Then he raped me!" She covered her face and sobbed.

Ray had no words. He stared at her, and the bits and pieces of information he had gleaned, the observations he had made, fell into place.

"You have to believe me, Ray. I had to tell somebody!"

"I know you're telling the truth, Rosa," he responded gently. "I'm sorry there was no one to protect you," Ray said as he knelt beside his sister. He took her hands in his and squeezed them reassuringly.

"It's all over now. You don't have to be afraid anymore," he said.

"I know," she said, "but I never really forgave him, and now I miss him, too. Is that awful?"

"No, Rosie. It's not awful, it's human. Remember that hat with the cherries on it?"

Rosa looked at her brother, her eyes brimming with tears.

"Try to remember those times and eventually your pain will go away," he said and brought her hands up to his lips.

"Ray? Do you think you might ever come home to live?" she asked.

"I don't think so," said Ray thoughtfully. "But I've been thinking about fixing up Grandpa's house to use for an office when I'm in Los Lunas. I could spend more time here that way."

"That would be so wonderful," said Rosa, the tears splashing even as she smiled.

"Look, Rosie. I've got to go to work but I'll come see you again, soon. I won't stay away, I promise. The next time we'll go for a ride in my new car. Would you like that?"

She smiled at her brother's effort to make her feel better.

"That would be nice," she said. "Maybe you'll let me drive it?"

"Maybe," said Ray.

"I'll be expecting you."

28.

RAY WAS WORKING FROM HOME the morning he had a surprise visit from Marcela. He hadn't seen her for more than a year and she'd done something to her hair. What once had been almost blue black was now frizzy and henna colored. It made her already pale features look even paler; almost ethereal. She wore black liner around her eyes, but her lips were glossed with a pale, nearly white-pink shade of lipstick. She walked right into his room without invitation.

"How have you been, Ray?" she asked, swaying her casually clad body as she walked about the room. "It's been ages, hasn't it?"

"How did you know where I live?" he asked her.

"What? Like it's a secret? The office you work for is listed in the Journal. I just took it from there," she said smugly.

Ray's first impulse was to yell at her, but she was so unpredictable that he didn't know what she'd do. He wasn't happy to see her because he knew there was a motive for her visit.

"What do you want?" he asked outright, not wanting to give her the benefit of the doubt.

"Well. . ." she laughed nervously, "what have you been doing with yourself?" She sat on his bed, and crossed her legs.

Ray didn't answer immediately. He was trying to maintain a calm exterior, because inside him, old feelings were beginning to stir. He had to concentrate on what he was saying to keep from stammering.

"Still working?" she asked, without waiting for him to answer.

He nodded, noticing a slight lisp in her speech for the first time.

He leaned with his back against the wall, turning to the side to look at her.

"Why are you here?" he asked.

"To visit an old friend," she said, barely lisping. She smiled at him.

"Come on," Ray said, tossing his head.

"What is it? You still mad?" The edge was gone from her voice and once again she was self-assured. "I make you nervous, don't I?"

"Look, Marcela. I've got things to do," said Ray impatiently, afraid that he was losing his grip.

"Remember the times back at UNM?" she asked.

"What about them?"

"I made you nervous then, too, didn't I?" Her voice sounded more confident.

"Just your imagination," Ray said, now a little defensive.

She smiled and lowered her eyelids at him.

"You know, a girl gets lonely for her friends, Ray. Do you ever get lonely?"

Ray looked away from her and stared straight ahead. She rose from the bed and walked to where he was standing. He didn't look at her.

"A boy could become a man very quickly in the city," she said, hovering close without touching him. "You know what I mean?"

He darted his head around to face her, and his carefully contained emotions flared. "You've been hanging around your *pachuco* friends too long!" He accused her of keeping bad company using the Mexican slang she understood.

"I knew it! You're still mad, aren't you? Isn't there anyway I could make it up to you?"

"Yeah!" he said, grabbing her by the arm and pulling her across the room. "You could get out of here!"

"But I'm not ready to leave yet," she said, freeing her arm and returning to stand by the bed.

"Get it straight, Marcela. I don't want anything to do with you!"

She turned her back to him and he threw his hands up in exasperation and withdrew.

"You know Ray, we could get to be friends," she said, and this time the quality of her voice was gentler.

He waited for her to say something else so he would have every excuse to throw her out. But she didn't speak. She began moving her hands up her sides, paused a moment with each hand on her hips, and with a flourish, turned around and pulled the sweater she wore over her head. Her uncovered bra-less breasts quivered against her body. She smiled.

Ray's reaction was involuntary and immediate. Without wasting words, he grabbed her by the arm and pulled her again towards the door. But half way there she balked, and he began struggling with her. He had to put his arms around her and pin her to him, to keep her from scratching him. As she turned in his grip, her round breasts kneaded against his chest. He couldn't hold her long, and when he let go, she stepped back from him but didn't try to escape.

Angry and excited, he couldn't trust his legs to hold him up. He went down on his knees, put his hands on his thighs and hung his head, turning his eyes up to look at her. She stared down at him a moment, then methodically removed her skirt and stood naked in front of him. He was powerless to move against her. His anger surged as he felt the need to punish her. He stood up again, fighting hard to control himself.

She began to laugh–a low animal sound erupting in soft, melodic spasms that whittled at his control. Then she took a step towards him. With impulsive force, he struck her across the face with his hand.

"Get out!" he said. She sprung at him in a frenzy of snarling and clawing, but he was too fast for her. Catching her by the wrists, they struggled, and fell onto the bed. He put his weight on her to hold her down. A small drop of blood appeared on her lip where he had struck her. She sank her teeth into the hard muscle of his shoulder and clung there. Pain shot up his neck and down his arm, and she suddenly had control of him by the force she put into her bite. Forced to free her arms, he pressed her down with his body, unwilling to give in so easily.

Immediately her arms went up around his neck in an embrace. She pulled open his shirt to expose the wounded area, and he braced to be bitten again. But it didn't happen. Instead, she put her lips gently against the skin, drew her tongue across the welts made by her teeth and tasted his skin. Helplessly, he submitted. He was still angry but now he was also aroused. He moved just enough to open his pants and pushed himself down on her, channeling his anger to the place where their bodies met. She gave way at first then slowly her body became taut. He could hardly tell that she was breathing. He thrust his body hungrily, needing to satisfy an urge he knew well, and she met him, absorbing the impact. She began breathing rapidly. A moan started out of her, so subtle that it reminded Ray of a pigeon's purling call. As the moan found its way out, it quavered plaintively before it rose and drifted. It was over in the span of a tense shudder, and his heat funneled into her. He collapsed and stayed where he was, gasping as though the air had turned to cotton.

Ray stayed beside Marcela on the bed, watching her breathe. She had done for him what no one else could; she relieved a pent-up tension that had dogged him since he was a teenager. His feelings over the death of his father, although not overt, had subtly eroded his confidence and left him feeling strangely alone. Now he was completely relaxed and felt like he could drift off to sleep. He could feel the heat rising from her naked body. It had a pleasant fragrance like peaches and he controlled the urge to kiss her shoulder. He became suddenly self-conscious about her nakedness, and carefully pulled the sheet up to her shoulders, staying as still as possible so as not to disturb her.

29.

THREE WEEKS HAD PASSED. Rosa was getting anxious to see her brother. She figured he was busy on a big assignment and had forgotten his promise to visit her. She was lonely, wanted to talk to someone who was family. She went about her chores, obsessively cleaning what had already been cleaned. Her day seemed never ending by late afternoon. She decided to drive into Albuquerque to see Ray. She had driven the truck into Albuquerque once before, when she went to see Miguel at the detention center. She also knew where Ray worked. She expected him to be working late on a Monday evening, so she would drive to meet him, just after work. She put on one of her nicer dresses, her newest pumps, dabbed on a bit of lipstick, and pulled a shawl from the drawer. She grabbed the keys to the truck, locking the house on her way out.

The truck started after a few pumps on the gas pedal. She revved the engine a couple of times to get it going, the way Pete had taught her. She headed out of town toward Albuquerque. The daylight seemed to be fading faster than she expected, so she turned on the headlights. By the time she reached the turnoff to what she thought was the way to Ray's office, she began to regret that she had been so impulsive. Everything looked the same in the fading light; the street signs were hard to see. Her instinct was to keep driving until she saw something familiar, but nothing did. She turned onto a street to the left, thinking she would go back to where she started. The street was one-way and led her to an intersection that confused her even more. She suspected she would end up going in circles if she didn't find her way to the main highway again. She looked around at the sky, trying to determine what direction to go. She could see the faint light of the western horizon to her left, the dark, looming Sandia Mountains far away to her right. She assumed the way back to the main road was west, so she took the street away from the mountains.

After driving past several streets, she saw the highway about a half-mile away. She stayed on course until she came to the intersection marking the route to I-25 South. She drove toward the exit, merged with the traffic, and felt relieved as she started her journey back home. Less than ten minutes later, the truck began to hesitate and lurch. She knew she should pull over, but didn't want to be stranded on the interstate. A few moments later, she pulled off at an exit just in time. The truck's engine stopped running. She was able to steer by putting in the clutch to keep it moving down the incline where it came to a stop on the right side of the road — a few yards from the intersection, barely off the pavement. She set the brake, turned the key, turned off the lights. She sat staring out at the faint glow in the western sky.

After all the things that had happened to her, Rosa had learned to be fearless. In all that time, she had never been alone and helpless like this. She had no way to contact anyone. There were no lights in the area where she had stopped — it was apparent no one lived nearby. She considered her options. If she stayed in the truck, she could lock the doors and sleep on the seat until morning, when someone was sure to spot her. On the other hand, she could lock the truck, start walking back toward town along what seemed to be a frontage road — at least she wouldn't be on the highway. Inclined toward action, she got out of the truck and looked around. She reached for her shawl, the truck keys, pushed down the button to lock the door, and slammed it shut. She started walking.

The frontage road was little more than a dirt road studded with bits of asphalt. It was overgrown with weeds along the sides, but it looked used. Rosa wrapped the shawl over her head, swung the long end over her shoulder, and began slowly walking north. She found it easier to see the ground once the moon began to rise. She heard rustling in the weeds that startled her a bit, but then recognized the quick scurry of a field mouse darting out from the brush. She kept walking, wishing she had worn more sensible shoes. She had gone about a half mile when she saw the headlights of a vehicle off in the distance coming toward her. She moved to the side of road and began waving. The vehicle slowed down as it approached, but the headlights were blinding and Rosa put her hand over her eyes. She could see the outline of a pickup in the haze of light as the vehicle stopped beside her. The door opened.

Rosa was so relieved that she began talking, quickly, nervously, about what had happened. She explained that she had been on her way to see her brother. Pointing behind her, she explained that her truck had run out of gas. She leaned into the open door, preparing to climb in, but hesitated, as there was no light inside the cab. Nervous, she laughed a little, thanking the stranger for his help, asking if he would mind driving her to the nearest gas station.

The driver shifted in his seat and ducked out of the shadow of the interior of the cab to get a better look at the hitchhiker. It was brighter outside, but the moon behind her obscured her face. He surveyed her clothing and high-heeled shoes, but he couldn't see her hair, because she wore a shawl over her head.

"Sure," he said. "Get in."

Rosa stepped onto the running board, swinging herself gracefully onto the seat. She reached for the door and closed it with a firm slam. She couldn't see the face of the man who was driving, but he seemed nice enough, so she felt no immediate cause for alarm. The driver continued along the road, as if there had been no interruption.

"You live in these parts?" asked Rosa.

"Not far," replied the driver.

"I'm from Los Lunas," said Rosa.

"Hmm," said the man.

"How far is the nearest gas station?" Rosa asked.

"A couple of miles," he replied.

"Have you got something to put gas in?"

"Sí, in the back there."

The man's response got Rosa's attention for the first time. His voice suddenly sounded familiar, but she just couldn't place it.

"That's it! That's my truck," said Rosa. Ahead in the distance, the silhouette of the truck became visible in the moonlight.

"I see it," he replied as he neared the vehicle. "It will still be there in the morning." He drove past the stranded vehicle, made a swift U-turn and drove in the opposite direction.

"Where are we going?" Rosa asked, suddenly apprehensive.

"Gas station is closer this way," replied the driver.

Rosa began to wonder what she had gotten herself into. The driver had a creepy way about him. He said very little and his face remained in the shadows of the truck's dark cab. She decided to take a more direct approach.

"What's your name? I'd like to know who to thank when I finally get home tonight." She felt him stir.

"Luis," he responded.

"Oh, that's my uncle's name," she said, cheering up.

"Yeah?" asked the man. "He lives around here?"

"No, he lives on the north end of Albuquerque."

"What does he do?"

"Honestly, I don't really know. But I think he has a job."

The conversation was making Rosa feel more relaxed, so she pulled the shawl from her head and let it fall around her shoulders. The moon had risen higher and was now casting a soft light into the truck where she sat. Her unruly hair formed a luminous halo around her face and the moonlight made her skin seem pale, ghostly. The man turned to look at her. She felt a cold shiver cross her neck and shoulders.

"Rosa?"

Rosa stared into the face of her uncle. The pickup jerked to a halt, tires skidding on the dirt. He reached up to the ceiling of the cab and flipped a switch that turned on the inside light.

"Tío!" Rosa said. "I had no idea it was you all this time. Why didn't you say something?"

"I didn't recognize you, Rosa. You're all grown up," said her uncle, as he gripped the steering wheel and looked away, clearly shaken.

"What in the world are you doing out here in the dark?" he asked her, as though he had not heard her earlier explanation. "You should be at home, safe in your bed."

"I can't believe that in this entire city, you are the one to find me. What sort of luck is that, Tío?

"It's the luck of angels," said her uncle, as he stared at her glowing face and tentatively reached to touch her hair. "Who would have thought that I would find you under these circumstances, Rosa de Castilla?"

Rosa smiled at hearing him use that nickname for her, after so long. His intimate gesture embarrassed her.

"I must take you home," he said. "Tomorrow, I'll bring a friend, some gas, and we'll get your truck home, too. That was your papá's truck, qué no?"

"It was his truck. I learned to drive it when Mama was sick so I could run errands. I forgot how much gas it uses, and here I am."

She made her uncle laugh. For a moment, she forgot he was the same Luis that made her nervous with his intense attention and suggestive hugs.

"I'm ready to go home, Tío."

"Very well," he replied, excited by the opportunity to look after his niece. "I'll make sure you get home safe and sound. You hear?" He drove the pickup to the next on-ramp, heading south towards Los Lunas. He began to whistle an old Mexican tune, El Corrido del Caballo Blanco. It was a favorite old ballad about a white stallion that made a long journey.

As the truck ate up the highway on her way home, Rosa felt relief. She thought about the events of the evening, the strange encounter with her uncle. She wondered what he was doing so far away from his home. The night air was cool and she pulled the shawl around her shoulders. Her uncle turned to look at her from time to time. He seemed happy. He was not the same person she had encountered when she first got into the pickup. When they reached her house, she felt safe with her uncle, but somehow realized that other women might not. She held that thought, as she waved goodbye to Luis from her doorstep.

30.

A WOMAN WAS WALKING her dog on the plateau just west of the subdivision where she lived. The wind usually blew dirt around out there, but the day was particularly calm and perfect for a walk. Her feet sank into the dry sand as she dodged some tumbleweeds and trash that had migrated there. The wind had leveled much of the area, but there was a bank of dirt that rose a few feet above the surface. It provided the woman with a higher view of her dog who sprinted down the bank and was sniffing every piece of trash, bush, stick and rock. She looked toward the south, raising her hand to shield her eyes then turned her attention back to the dog. He seemed to be interested in something and was digging and sniffing as he uncovered it. The woman called to him in an attempt to get his attention, but the dog persisted. She backtracked to where the bank leveled off to meet the surrounding surface and briskly walked to where her dog was digging.

At first sight the woman recognized the dog's discovery as a bone, probably from a dog or a deer. It was a disgusting thought but she knew that people often dumped dead animals or deer-hunting remains in that place, so she wasn't surprised. As the dog unearthed the rest of the bone, the woman stooped down for closer inspection and recognized the bone as a human femur. It had that unmistakable ball on one end that, had it been attached to a body, would fit into the hip socket. She was immediately concerned that she might have stepped into an Indian burial site. New Mexico, after all, is one of those places where the Indians' ancestors lived and roamed far and wide. It was inevitable that an ancient burial site would eventually be found where least expected, adding to the fear and frustration of contractors, whose plans to develop large tracts of land like this area could be stopped because of it.

A thought occurred to her. Indian burial site remains were usually dark and somewhat fossilized. This bone did not appear to be very old. It was possible that the bone belonged to a body that was dumped there. She felt a sense of dread creep into her as she attached the leash to the dog so she could pull him away from his prize. She took a deep breath, reached into the pocket of her jeans for her cell phone and called the police.

THE END

Epilogue

The area of the West Mesa remained undeveloped for years because the developer ran into complications and lacked money to build there. It was instead used by people making illegal runs at night to dump trash and garden refuse to avoid paying for the legitimate use of the landfill. People came and went unnoticed because they entered that desolate area after midnight, mostly because no one cared about the sandy, weedy acreage where the winds generated dunes and dust devils that obliterated and reshaped the landscape.

The discovery of a single bone led to the unearthing of eleven bodies buried in shallow graves on the mesa. The graves became a crime scene investigation that lasted months. Body after body was uncovered, each in an individual grave as the Mesa gave up its grisly cache within yards of a thriving housing development. The decomposed bodies were all female and one contained a fetus. One of the women was an African American not from New Mexico. The remains included little clothing that could give authorities clues as to what the victims did for a living. DNA proved to be the only way to tell their true identities. Police held back information that they hoped would serve to eventually catch the killer.

The murders were in the news nearly every night for weeks. But they dropped to once a month as the investigation continued. The pictures of the victims and family interviews began appearing on the news as soon as the DNA results started coming in. Law Enforcement detectives and FBI profilers continued to work with investigators to solve the series of murders without any witnesses or much forensic evidence. Notices went out asking the public for information that might shed light on the case, but people abused the opportunity by suggesting as suspects their old boyfriends or family members who were giving them grief.

There have been suspects, leads and tips since the women were discovered, but the murderer has not been identified. Interest in solving the case seems to have faded, but the souls of eleven women and an infant continue to haunt the city, waiting to tell the story about how they died and who killed them.

As this book goes into release, it is the author's hope that the case will finally be solved and justice served for the victims.